PARANORMAL COZY MYSTERY

Hopes & Slippery Slopes

TRIXIE SILVERTALE

Sittin' On A Goldmine
Productions L.L.C.

Sittin' On A Goldmine Productions, L.L.C.

info@sittinonagoldmine.co

www.sittinonagoldmine.co

Publisher's note: This is a work of fiction. Names, characters, places and incidents are products of the author's imagination or are used fictitiously and are not to be construed as real. Any resemblance to actual events, locales, organizations, or persons, living or dead, is entirely coincidental.

ISBN: 978-1-952739-02-6

Cover Design © Sittin' On A Goldmine Productions, L.L.C.

Trixie Silvertale
Hopes and Slippery Slopes: Paranormal Cozy Mystery : a novel / by Trixie Silvertale — 1st ed.
[1. Paranormal Cozy Mystery — Fiction. 2. Cozy Mystery — Fiction. 3. Amateur Sleuths — Fiction. 4. Female Sleuth — Fiction. 5. Wit and Humor — Fiction.] 1. Title.

CHAPTER 1

THE DARK TENDRILS of dreamland refuse to loosen their hold. I can't shake the weight of dread following me back to consciousness. What I need is some of that fresh air everyone raves about and massive quantities of java. Time to get this rig rolling.

Outside the Bell, Book & Candle, I squint my eyes against the bright sun and walk through little clouds of my own breath as I meander down Main Street toward Myrtle's Diner. Behind my shop, the great lake resting in the harbor of the town that tech forgot is, at long last, cloaked in white.

Born and raised in Arizona, I never imagined living in a place like Pin Cherry Harbor. Of course, the old me was too consumed with trying to make ends meet on a broke barista's salary to have dreams. I ran with a gaggle of fake friends and bounced down a list of insincere, unworthy boyfriends.

Today, the new me gets to enjoy my favorite breakfast, with a good-hearted, gorgeous man, at an amazing diner named after my dearly departed grandmother and operated by my surrogate grandpa.

An entire string of words that little orphan Mitzy never imagined uttering. Tragically losing my mother at eleven and churning my way through a series of mostly unsavory foster homes left me underwhelmed and expecting little from life.

But when a mysterious old man with a marvelous mustache knocked on the door of my should-be-condemned apartment and handed me a manila envelope holding an unbelievable new future, my world literally flipped upside down and inside out.

The malodorous bus that ferried me across the country to almost-Canada certainly disguised the hidden potential in my sudden relocation.

Now I have a philanthropic foundation, a fascinating three-story bookshop and printing museum, a surprise father, an annoyingly endearing feline, a wonderful but interfering Ghost-ma—and did I mention the kind and handsome boyfriend?

The warm welcome of Myrtle's Diner envelops me, and I wave to Odell as he gives me the standard spatula salute through the red-Formica-trimmed orders-up window.

Sheriff Erick Harper occupies the booth in the corner, and his inviting smile melts my heart.

I slide onto the bench seat opposite him, and the flame-red bun of the best waitress in town appears beside me.

"Morning, Mitzy." She slides a mug of coffee onto the table and checks to make sure I have enough individual creamers in the pale-green melamine bowl.

"Good morning, Tally. How is your brother doing?"

She smiles proudly. "He's got the whole veterinary clinic retrofitted now. He can conduct examinations, surgeries, and even run the front desk from his wheelchair."

"That's wonderful. He's hands-down the best vet in Birch County. I'm glad he was able to work things out." We exchange a knowing look, and neither of us wants to mention the horrible hit-and-run accident that left her brother paralyzed. That's another story.

Erick reaches across the table and grabs my hand, sending tingles up my arm. "We sure were lucky to have Mitzy Moon on that case, wouldn't you say, Tally?"

She nods fervently. "From your mouth to God's ears, Sheriff."

I shake my head and flush with embarrassment.

Tally whisks away to see to the handful of other customers, and Odell approaches with our breakfasts.

I kind of love coming to a place like this. No need to order. Just sit back and wait to have exactly what you didn't know you wanted, but absolutely needed, delivered.

Odell slides a stack of pancakes in front of Erick and I get a plate of scrambled eggs with chorizo, golden home fries, and a bottle of Tabasco. He slips a small side-plate bearing an English muffin on the table and I look up in confusion.

The lines in his weathered face deepen and his eyes twinkle as he grins. "Figured you'd better carbo-load. It's gonna be a mighty long, chilly day at the races." He raps his knuckles twice on the table and returns to the kitchen.

"If you say so. Smells delicious," I call after him.

Erick nods. "That's right. You and your dad are headed out to the snocross today."

Having already shoved an enormous forkful of home fries into my mouth, I return the nod, and grin.

He chuckles. "Don't let me interrupt your breakfast, Moon."

I wash it all down with a swig of black gold. "Oh, don't worry, I never would."

His blue eyes dance with delight, and a satisfied silence settles over the table while we tuck into our meals.

I'm not ashamed to say, I finish first. "Let me regale you with the latest gossip while you finish your breakfast, slowpoke."

His head shakes with laughter and a little swath of his beautiful blond hair swings loose from his pomade.

And I thought my *breakfast* was yummy! Fortunately, I've learned to keep thoughts like that safely locked in my head—most of the time. Instead, I turn to the event on everyone's mind. "Did you receive your invitation to my dad's wedding?"

He nods and politely swallows his food before answering. "Yes. An outdoor wedding on New Year's Eve! I'm looking into parkas and sled dogs as we speak."

We share a snicker. "You're not allowed to raise a single complaint. This is Amaryllis's wedding, and she's allowed to take off her corporate lawyer hat for a minute and indulge in a winter fantasy. Her day, her way. Plus, it's just the reception that's outdoors. According to my dad, the ceremony is going to be inside my bookshop."

Erick shrugs. "If you say so. The town's not that

big. I'm sure everyone will end up at the right place."

"So you're not going to the races?"

He pushes his bottom lip up and shakes his head. "Not unless there's a riot. I have a mountain of paperwork and a whole county to monitor. The drag races may be noisy, but they're generally quite civilized. Good group of guys that just enjoy going fast."

"I can respect that." I reach for my cup of wake-up juice, but stop mid-motion.

Erick leans across the table and lowers his voice. "Really? Because if memory serves, you're the girl who wanted to take it *slow*. But if you're ready to speed things up . . . I'm your guy."

Tingly shivers run up and down my spine and my belly flip-flops. I definitely have to remember never to play poker with this man. He's far too ready to call my bluff.

A boisterous group of eight to ten men burst into the café and stomp the slush off their boots. They fill two booths and one of the four-tops by the front window.

Tally swoops in with menus and mugs, and makes small talk.

"You folks here for the snocross?"

"Oh yeah, you betcha. I got two boys runnin' in the junior and junior novice divisions."

Tally nods, and another red-cheeked patron pipes up. "My daughter's running in the junior novice division, and she's gonna take that title with one hand tied behind her back."

A heated but friendly debate ensues.

Erick walks his fingers across the table and turns his palm upward.

I slip my hand into his and he gives it a little squeeze. "See, they're passionate but respectful. I'm sure you and your father will have a great day. Dress warm and be sure to take earmuffs."

"Earmuffs? I have a stocking cap. Isn't that enough?"

He shakes his head and furrows his brow. "Trust me, you're gonna want the earmuffs."

Rolling my eyes, I slide out of the booth. "Thanks for breakfast, Sheriff. I better get back and see what Gra— great ol' Twiggy needs before I head out." My eyes are saucers, and I hope he didn't notice my almost slip.

"One day, you're going to finish that sentence, Moon. I promise you." He polishes his badge with his knuckles and narrows his gaze teasingly.

I choke on a nervous giggle, bus my dishes, and wave to Odell as I leave.

Tramping back down Main Street toward my bookstore, I smack a mittened hand on my own forehead. I really need to stop almost talking about my supposedly dead grandmother in front of my highly observant boyfriend.

Gripping the handle on the intricately carved wooden door, I smirk at the figure that so closely resembles my present day wildcat. I'm not the only one with secrets, am I, Pyewacket?

Pulling open the door, I brush through the quiet stacks and run my fingers along a row of novels. Some days it's hard to believe that this whole book-filled place, from thick carpets to tin-plated ceiling, is mine. I step over the "No Admittance" chain at the bottom of the wrought-iron spiral staircase and head up to the second-floor mezzanine.

The Rare Books Loft is strictly off-limits to patrons, except for one day a month, when scholarly research is allowed by appointment only. I still don't understand the full value of what I possess, but as I tread across the loft between the neat rows of oak tables, each with their brass reading lamps and delicate green-glass shades, a warm feeling of home wells up inside.

I turn and stretch my arms out, mimicking the curve of the balconies extending on either side of the mezzanine. There used to be huge fermentation tanks on the first floor of this famous brewery. My grandpa Cal bought the historic landmark for my grandmother, and she spent her entire life converting it into this magnificent bookstore and printing museum.

Inhaling the scent of age-old mysteries, I abandon the view and approach the secret door to my apartment. Reaching up to the candle sconce, next to my special copy of *Saducismus Triumphatus*, I tilt it down and the bookcase door slides open.

The ghost of Myrtle Isadora swooshes out of the closet with glee. "Good, you're back. I've got the perfect thing laid out for you to wear. Plenty of layers, and those special boots I was telling you about."

"Good morning to you too, Grams."

Her apparition shimmers, and she places a bejeweled fist on one hip as she smooths the folds of her burgundy silk-and-tulle Marchesa burial gown. "Don't take that tone with me, young lady. You'll be thanking me when you're out there freezing your ample behind off on the mountain."

"Far be it from me to argue with a fashion expert such as yourself."

She flutters her translucent eyelashes and giggles. "Sass all you want. You know I'm right."

Heading into the closet I've nicknamed *Sex and the City* meets *Confessions of a Shopaholic*, I'm pleased to see that today's outfit does not include high heels. There's at least one big check mark in the "pros" column for snocross.

"Don't you worry, dear, I'll be sure to pick out a nice pair of Christian Louboutin's for your wedding attire."

I point a sharp finger toward my lips. "Grams! You know the rules about thought-dropping! If these lips aren't moving, you don't get to comment."

She throws her ethereal limbs into the air. "Not even in defense of fashion?"

"Especially not for that." I begin the arduous process of layering my silk long underwear and wool socks underneath the rest of the garb Ghost-ma has selected. "Where's Pyewacket?"

"I haven't seen him this morning. He may be patrolling in the museum. The mice tend to be rather active indoors this time of year."

"Ew."

"Mr. Cuddlekins always earns his keep."

I chuckle at her fierce defense of the furry fiend and finish my transformation into a polar explorer. "Well, it looks like I'm ready to conquer Antarctica!"

"Mitzy. You're such a hoot! You have fun with your dad today and be sure to thank him for agreeing to get married in the bookshop. You know how much it means to me."

"I will, Grams." As I circle down the treads to the first floor it occurs to me that Isadora always got her way in life, and not a whole lot has changed in death.

A voice from the ether whispers, "I heard that."

"Get out of my head, woman!"

A patron in the historical mysteries section looks up in confusion.

My expression mirrors her shock. Despite owning a bookshop, customers here are an especially rare sight. I smile self-consciously and rush toward the glowing red EXIT sign above the door leading into the alleyway between my building and my father's.

CHAPTER 2

HAVING MY OWN key to my father's place across the alley is convenient, but it's still a little unsettling to be creeping around the big empty building on the weekend. We exchanged keys for convenience and safety, and also because I'm not quite ready to connect our two buildings with the Frida Kahlo/Diego Rivera style walkway that my father keeps proposing.

The impressive Duncan Restorative Justice Foundation is a miniature replica of the most famous building in all of Birch County: City Hall. A picture-perfect structure that always reminds me of a scene from *To Kill a Mockingbird*. The original, in the town square, stands about fifty feet tall. Three stories of solid granite with copper parapet walls, featuring original terrazzo floors, ornamental plaster cornices, and marble walls at the elevator lobby. It's truly the height of architectural design in Pin Cherry. My dad didn't miss a detail when he recreated the lavish, yet slightly miniaturized, version of the architecture for his headquarters.

He may have spent fifteen regrettable years in Clearwater State Pen for a crime he mostly didn't commit, but he definitely used the experience to turn his life around. His foundation provides a legal defense fund for wrongly convicted prisoners and a job placement resource for ex-cons.

Walking toward the life-size statue of the grandfather I never had the opportunity to meet, I stop and read the dedication plaque for the first time.

In memory of Calvin Jacob Duncan

Father, husband, and grandfather

May his efforts to protect the town he built, with jobs and commerce, via the Midwest Union Railway, and his love for his family, remain his undying legacy. It's never too late to choose love.

I dab at the tears under my eyes with my woolen mittens, before removing them and shoving them in the pocket of my puffy coat. I wish my dad could've had a chance to hear about grandpa Cal's change of heart before his untimely death, but, like so many of the relationships in the Duncan family tree, the truths revealed after the fact seem to build bonds that last beyond the veil. They may have had a terrible falling out in life, but Grandpa Cal uncovered the truth and changed his will. That act cost him his life, but it went a long way to healing the rift with his son, and laying the groundwork for my chance at a better relationship with my dad.

Continuing into the marble enclosed elevator lobby, I drop my defenses a fraction of an inch and let myself bask in the warmth of family as I ascend.

PING. The elevator doors slide open and I find myself right in the middle of an argument.

So much for the family-love vibe. "Um, should I come back later, Dad?"

Two guilty faces spin toward me, and my father runs a nervous hand through his ice-blond hair, but it's his fiancée who comes to our rescue.

Amaryllis smiles and shrugs her petite shoulders. "Don't worry, Mitzy, it's not a real argument. Your father is trying to convince me to go to the snowmobile drag races today. However, while I'm extremely proud of my soon-to-be husband and his record number of Junior Snocross Champion titles, my schedule is overflowing with wedding-planning duties."

She arches an eyebrow, and the golden flecks in her brown eyes sparkle as she gives me a conspiratorial wink.

I tug my stocking cap off, shake out the bone-white hair I inherited from my father, and breathe a sigh of relief. "Look, Dad, she's right. You and I can manage the races. You can present the trophies, or whatever, and Amaryllis can take care of the wedding stuff. New Year's Eve is coming up fast, and I don't know very much about weddings and even less about winter, but it seems to me that it will take quite a bit of preparation to keep your guests from straight up freezing to death at an outdoor reception!"

Amaryllis chuckles as she refills her coffee cup. "I keep telling Jacob that it's more complicated to plan a wedding than he thinks. But you know men!" She imitates my father's voice and jokes, "Just tell me what to wear and when to be there." She laughs and rolls her eyes. "That's his mantra."

My dad covers his face with one large, strong hand and offers no defense.

She pours another cup of coffee, adds a splash of Irish cream, and flashes her eyebrows as she hands it to me. "You'll need that extra kick to keep you warm. You're going to be surprised by what it feels like to be outdoors in the heart of winter at near-zero temps for an entire day."

I grasp the mug of liquid alert and inhale the comforting aroma. "At least you don't have to pay for a wedding venue. I mean, I wasn't planning on charging you for the bookshop." My hilarious comment meets with crickets.

My father shakes his head, and his eyes widen in fear as an uncomfortable silence grows.

Amaryllis sets her mug on the black granite countertop and transfers a hand to her hip. "Jacob Duncan, is there something you're not telling me?"

My dad and I exchange a worried glance.

He takes the lead. "My mom was hoping—always hoped—that I'd be married in the bookshop."

She narrows her gaze and scans the unspoken exchange between my father and me. "I may not be litigating cases in a courtroom, now that I'm official counsel for the Duncan Restorative Justice Foundation, but I haven't lost my ability to read people. You two are hiding something, and you're not leaving this penthouse until I find out what it is. Why you would wait until the last minute to drop this in my lap, Jacob, is beyond me."

My dad's moose-sized shoulders sag appreciably. "It's not important."

The hairs on the back of my neck tingle and the magicked mood ring on my left hand delivers an icy chill which creeps up my arm at a deliberate pace.

Her eyes widen with concern, and she walks around the counter to slip an arm around my father's waist. "Jacob, something really is wrong, isn't it? I thought we agreed to have no secrets. A lawyer marrying an ex-con is scandalous enough, but I understand what led you to commit the robbery—and they framed you for the murder. You served your time—and then some—and paid your debt to society. What else is there? I can't imagine there's anything worse?" Her voice shakes, but her eyes are full of compassion.

Little beads of sweat pop out along my father's brow.

My psychic senses deliver a volley of highly charged messages. Doing my best to ignore all supernatural information, I shift my weight from one foot to the other, cross my arms, and pretend to admire the artwork on the wall.

Amaryllis pulls away from my dad, and her expression grows cold. "Listen, you two, no secrets means no secrets. I've dreamt of getting married on New Year's Eve since I was a little girl, but I will cancel the Veuve Clicquot order and put this entire thing on hold until I get to the truth. Reality is far more important to me than a childhood fantasy."

Jacob looks at me, and his eyes beg for forgiveness.

My entire body vibrates with fear as I shake my head in warning.

He takes a deep breath and launches into his explanation. "Amaryllis, honey, my mother's ghost lives in the bookshop. Mitzy can see ghosts. And talk to them. And my mom wants us to get married there. I know it sounds crazy, but you have to be-lieve me."

The stern look on her face vanishes, and a slow smile lifts her heart-shaped mouth as a single tear trickles down her cheek. She closes the distance between us and hugs me tightly. "I knew it! I knew you had the gift, Mitzy. You remember that time— Never mind." Turning to my father, she offers him absolution. "Of course we'll get married in the bookshop, Jacob. You'll be astonished at what I can accomplish in a week! I can redirect the vendors and put a notice in the paper to alert the guests to the change. Easy peasy." She squeezes me one more time and the love in her eyes nearly breaks my heart. "Mizithra, I know I can never replace your mother, but I hope you'll let me try."

Now I'm crying. "You don't think I'm a freak? I mean, it's not every day you meet someone who talks to ghosts."

"I always knew you were special. How can any child of Jacob Duncan's be anything less than extraordinary? Do you think Twiggy will assist me in getting things sorted for the ceremony?"

The belly laugh that grips me comes out of nowhere. "I think you mean, can *you* assist Twiggy?"

We all share a hearty chuckle at the thought of anyone telling Twiggy what to do.

My volunteer employee, Twiggy, was my grandmother's best friend in life and currently runs the bookshop for me, while refusing any form of payment other than my, generally public, embarrassments. Part of me is sure she would take a bullet for me, but until that moment comes, she'd much prefer to laugh at my natural clumsiness and relationship foibles.

My father wipes his forehead and exhales loudly. "Whew! That's a load off. Trust me, Snugglebear, I didn't enjoy keeping that secret." Jacob breathes deeply and squares his relieved shoulders. "Even though it wasn't really mine to tell, hopefully my amazing and brilliant daughter will forgive me."

His big grey eyes stare pleadingly into mine and I shrug. "Flattery will get you everywhere, Dad. I may not be strong enough to tell Erick about it yet, but now that Amaryllis is part of the family, I think she deserves to know the truth."

She places a hand on my arm. "You haven't told Erick? I thought you two were getting rather serious?"

Fidgeting and staring at the floor, I avoid a direct response. "Things are fine. I'm taking it slow. I made a lot of bad choices in my past, and I kinda hope things work out with him—long-term. You know?"

Her gaze immediately drifts to my father and they exchange a heart-melting eye-hug. "I know exactly what you mean."

Oh brother. Snugglebears and eye-hugs! This is way too much mushy stuff this early in the morning. I'm not entirely comfortable baring all my emotions for anyone, and I certainly don't need to watch someone else do it. Time to get this train out of the station. "We better get going. I don't want Dad to be late for his runway walk!"

Amaryllis laughs so hard she snorts. "All hail the King of Snocross."

My dad shakes his head in mock frustration, but he takes the hint.

As the elevator descends, he slips an arm around my shoulders, leans down, and kisses the top of my head. "Thanks for letting me bring her into the inner circle, sweetie. I know we can trust her."

"Yeah, I feel that way too." In the alleyway between my father's foundation/penthouse and my bookshop, a thick layer of snow blankets the ground, nearly hiding my earlier boot prints, and the gently falling flakes create a fairytale wrapped in a hushed mystery.

I insist on taking my Jeep, because it has better heating than my dad's 1950s pickup, but he insists on driving, since I'm a bit of an amateur in the snow.

"Far be it from me to argue with the eight-time Junior Snocross and Drag Race Champion!"

He scoffs and shakes his head in embarrassment.

CHAPTER 3

THE EARLY MORNING drive out to the old Fox
Mountain Ski Resort is as beautiful as a Hallmark
movie's midwinter sleigh ride. The thick flakes are
falling in earnest, and the windshield wipers swipe
them away with a rhythm all their own. Luckily, the
deer moving toward shelter in the deep pine and
birch forest stand out starkly against the folds of
white.

"Nice driving, Duncan."

My father replies with a sing-songy lilt. "Thank
you kindly." He takes the last sloping turn on the
winding road and pulls into one of the few available
spots.

The parking lot is packed with vehicles, trailers,
and pop-up tents. "Holy *Snow Day*! I think you un-
dersold this, Dad."

"Well, the winter is long and the residents of Pin Cherry Harbor are mighty creative."

I tug my hat down over my ears, and make sure my scarf is tucked inside my jacket, before slipping my wool mittens inside bigger leather mittens called choppers, if I'm remembering that correctly, and bravely step out of the Jeep. I barely make it four steps when I skid on a patch of ice, hidden beneath the fresh snowfall, and land on my well-padded backside.

My father comes to my rescue in a flash and helps me to my feet. "How about you hang on to me until we get you to the grandstand?"

"Grandstand? Like actual stacked seating where more than five or ten people will be watching?" I grip his arm and shake my head in awe.

"The ski resort is closed for renovations, Mitzy. What did you think all these cars were here for?"

"Copy that." As a film-school dropout, new experiences always tend to fall into one of three categories: blockbuster, box office flop, or cult classic. The jury's still out on this event, but one thing it does not lack is volume.

The engines are whining in well over fifty sleds. That's the cool insider name for snowmobiles, in case you live south of the Mason-Dixon line. At least a hundred sleds are being removed from trailers, revving up for no reason, or whipping around the brightly lit track, on what I can only assume are test laps.

According to my father's brief lesson during our car ride to the competition, there are two categories, with divisions for several age groups. There's snocross, which is a lot like motocross, but with snowmobiles on a hilly snow-packed oval track. There are also a day's worth of snowmobile drag races, which sounds similar to quarter-mile time trials, but once again, in the snow and going uphill. Snowmobiles can reach speeds of one hundred and fifty miles per hour in the drag races, so the uphill configuration allows for a safe cool down path. All I can think of is how much I wish I'd listened to Erick and added a pair of earmuffs to my outfit, to dampen the whine of the two-stroke engines.

"Duncan! Jacob Duncan!" A small man in a bright-orange parka and a fluorescent-green neck gaiter waves both of his arms wildly.

I elbow my dad and nod toward the shenanigans.

He leans down and whispers, "That will be the mayor. Looks like my official duties are about to begin. You get yourself some hot chocolate and a spot in the grandstand. Try to find a seat on the first row or two. The view is better from the top, but so is the windchill."

"Copy that, Champ."

His shoulders shake with laughter as he walks toward the mayor.

Hopping into the hot chocolate queue, I wonder if they sell it in pints? Maybe if I sip on a steady stream of warm chocolate goodness, I can survive the frigid festivities.

Although, as I take in the rows of porta-potties along the outskirts of the temporary race venue, I come to terms with the realities of weighing my warmth against my eventual need to relieve myself in the certain-to-be frosty facilities. Maybe a small cup of hot chocolate is the better plan, and I'll keep moving to stay alive.

The guy behind me in line offers a friendly smile and starts a conversation I didn't know I'd be having. "Spectator or racer?"

While I'm flattered that he thinks I might be able to handle a snowmobile, I don't know nearly enough about the sport to make any false claims. "Absolutely a spectator. I'm just here to support my dad."

"Nice. Your dad runnin' in the snocross or the drags?"

"Oh, he's not racing today. He's presenting some awards and probably other stuff."

"Wow. I didn't know I was in the presence of snocross royalty." He bows and lifts one eyebrow. "You're Jacob Duncan's kid?"

I'm not sure how I feel about being referred to as a "kid," but I'm not here to make a scene. "Yep. Eight-time Junior Snocross Champion."

The guy whoops and nods in admiration. "Actually, he was three-time Junior Snocross Champ, two-time Junior Stock Drags Champ, two-time Junior Modified Drags Champ, and one-time overall King of the Winter Circuit."

My eyes widen and I bite hard into my tongue to keep from cracking up. "Wow. He really was the king, huh?"

Ignoring my comment, the guy shouts to his friends, "Bristol, AJ, Eli, this here's Duncan's kid." He gestures frantically with his high-tech articulated leather gloves.

What is happening? My throat tightens and I instinctively step back.

Three fresh faces join the crowd and a mother in line behind us, with two young children, mutters something about manners and cutting in line.

"Excuse me, miss, why don't you and your kids go ahead of us?"

Her face flushes with guilt. Clearly she thought her comment was subsonic. I can't honestly be sure whether I heard it with my five regular senses or if my clairaudience delivered the message. Either way, she herds her pack ahead of us while my new friend brings the group up to speed with exaggerated tales of the amazing Jacob Duncan.

One of the newcomers nods his ski-mask-covered face in my direction and rolls up the part covering his face. "So, you here for the whole day?"

I shrug. "I'm here as long as my dad's here. I suppose the trophies don't get handed out until the end of the day, so probably, yes?"

The additional trio calls out in rapid succession.

"Cool."

"Sweet."

"Noice."

The group's original spokesperson thrusts out a mittened hand. "I'm Crank. This beast is AJ, the little guy Eli won junior drags last year and he's already the number three seed in the pro-stock drags this season, and Bristol's fourth in the women's snocross circuit. Points-wise, I mean."

Good thing he clarified. Because? I take a moment to remind myself that the universe brought me here for my pops, and not to *snark*, before I reply. "Nice to meet all of you. I'm Mitzy Moon. My—"

Bristol steps forward, pulls off her jester-style beanie, and takes a knee. "Dude, I'm your humble servant. I read a bunch of stories about you online and all the, like, mysteries you solved and stuff. You're my hero. For reals."

The others nod in agreement, and it would appear my sleuthing has eclipsed my father's championship status. Even though this strange meet up is turning out better than I anticipated, I'm eager to duck out of the spotlight and melt into the crowd. "Hey, forget about it. I just do what I can to help out, you know? Today is all about snowmobiles and my dad, all right?"

Bristol jumps to her feet. "No doubt. No doubt. If I win, though, I'm gonna full on dedicate my trophy to you."

"Thanks." It comes out as more of a question than I intended, but this tough snocross fangirl is throwing me off my game.

AJ and Eli snicker and jab elbows back and forth, and the super-sized AJ nearly knocks Eli off his feet. The small racer drops his decal-covered helmet and immediately retrieves it. He busies himself wiping off the snow covering his sponsors' logos.

Crank is not a guy to take a hint. "Where you sittin'? You can totally hang with us. I'm here as support crew, but it's truly cool if you want to hang out in the pits, you know, learn all the behind-the-scenes stuff from a top mechanic."

And he's humble, too. "Thanks, that's a super sweet offer, but I kinda promised my dad I'd be there for him, in case he needed anything. So, you guys go tune-up your sleds, and good luck. I'll be rooting for you, for sure."

This time the whole quartet sounds off.

"Cool."

"Sweet."

"Noice."

"Awesome, man." Crank gives me a "guy nod" before slugging AJ playfully.

The foursome tramp off toward the din of revving snowmobiles, and I breathe a sigh of relief.

Time to get back in that hot cocoa line and see if I can come up a winner.

"Mitzy. Mitzy, come on over here. I want you to meet someone." My father beckons me toward a running snowmobile, saddled with a rider in a full-face helmet with the visor pushed up.

Looks like it's going to be a "no joy" on the hot chocolate. I hustle to my dad's side and he wraps a friendly arm around my shoulder.

"Mitzy, this is Trey Lee. He's top seed in the current points standing in the pro-stock division and Mr. Jablonski coaches him."

I reach out and give the young rider a fist bump. "Jablonski? The taxidermist?"

The kid nods his helmet up and down. "Yeah, Coach Jawbone is the best. I'd never be top seed without him, you know?"

I have no intention of telling him that I do not

know. My only interaction with the creepy taxidermist left my skin crawling and my feet racing to put distance between us. "Oh, sure. That's great that he's coaching you. Does his son ride? Does he coach anyone else?"

Both my father and Trey scoff openly.

My dad pats Trey on the back and nods toward the pits. "You better get your sled checked out. I'm sure Coach will be here any minute."

Trey flicks his visor down, revs the snowmobile so hard it wheelies, and heads into the pits.

"The taxidermist is a snowmobile coach?"

My father's eyes drift to a faraway place in his memory. "Yeah, he was a champion on the circuit, and the second he retired, your grandpa Cal paid him a fortune to coach me."

My eyebrows arch under my stocking cap. "He was your coach? He coached the king of the slopes?" I can no longer contain my laughter, and my father's cheeks redden with more than the bite of winter.

"I deserved that. I was pretty full of myself back then. Jablonski was pushing me to move out of the junior division and go for the bigger prize money on the pro circuit. That was about the time my rebellious streak kicked in."

A knowing sensation of dread floods over me. "You and Cal didn't get along."

He leans away, and for a moment Jacob looks a little surprised. "Oh, right. Your psychic messages."

"As Pyewacket would say, 'can confirm'."

He walks toward the grandstand, and as I follow he compresses the catalyst of his fall from grace into a few brief sentences.

"Cal never came to any of the races. He wanted to brag about me in boardrooms and country clubs, but he never spent any time with me. He put all my prize money in a trust and wouldn't let me touch it. So, once I was king of the circuit, I quit. Jablonski was furious and didn't coach anyone else for almost five years. I started spending most of my spare time with less desirables—"

"Like Darrin?"

"Like Darrin." Jacob shakes his head and stares at the ground. "After his dishonorable discharge from the Navy and my dropping out of college, we started to plan the robbery."

We stop next to the grandstand and he hugs me tight.

The emotions are bubbling close to the surface, and I need to stuff them back down. "Cut to—amazing father and daughter reunion, and the king of the circuit is back to hand out trophies!"

Jacob chuckles and pats me on the back. "Grab those open seats on the second bench. I gotta check in with the mayor, but I should be able to join you for the first few drag races. The snocross doesn't start until later this afternoon."

"Here's to the races, Duncan."

My father wanders off, and I thread through the blankets, coolers, and children's games of chase, to take a seat in the second row.

The junior novice drag race is up first, and the small snowmobiles and young riders force me to wonder what kind of a dumpster fire I'm about to witness. Despite their stature, these eleven- to thirteen-year-old guys and gals know how to get it done. I'm surprised by the control they have over their sleds. One little guy even pops a wheelie like the big boys.

Asking the parka-encased human next to me to save my seat, I wander off to get some hot chocolate. Finally successful, I return to my seat in time for the pro-stock drags.

Each sled and rider is accompanied to the starting line by one support crewmember. I recognize Crank behind the sled on the far right and assume that Eli is at the helm of that snowmachine. The rider closest to the grandstands is the favorite, Trey, but he doesn't have a crewmember at his side. Maybe it's one of Coach Jawbone's rules.

The announcer's voice crackles to life. "Hang on to your seat cushions! This is the most talked about race of the day! Number one seed Trey Lee is here to protect his pro-stock title, and Eli McGrail is here to take it away!"

The riders rev their engines and plant their feet firmly on the running boards. Support crews take their cue to step behind the protective wall and the light tree blinks down.

Yellow. Yellow. Yellow. GREEN!

The roar is deafening!

"And they're off and running!"

All six sleds rear back into powerful wheelies and rocket down the track.

"Lee fights for the lead. McGrail is only a ski behind," the announcer shouts.

The crowd cheers and stomps their boots.

The entire grandstand shakes.

"Looks like Wiggins is fighting for control of—" The announcer stops in mid call.

The rider in lane two loses control of his sled and crashes into Trey.

"Wiggins flips his sled! Lee is forced off the track!"

Trey's sled skids off the groomed track and careens into the tree line.

I search the starting line for his coach, but I'm not sure I could identify Jablonski covered in layers of winter gear.

However, I do recognize my dad running up the slope.

I hop over the railing, into the snow, and follow. "Dad! Is he okay? Is he moving?"

My father moves like a charging bear. He leaps off the groomed track and pushes through the waist-deep snow amongst the trees.

Medics and a couple of mechanics from other crews are finally catching on. My father shouts instructions down the hill. "Get a stretcher. Trey's not moving! And somebody get a winch up here for this sled."

I stop at the edge of the groomed track, not confident enough to follow my father into the sinkhole of snow. "Dad, what can I do?"

He looks up from his perch next to the crumpled body of the young boy and whispers, "Is he alive? Are you getting any messages?"

I reach out with my psychic senses, and a sickening knot tightens in my stomach. Before I can share my message, other people arrive on scene and push past me to attach the winch's hook to the back of the sled.

The announcer is droning on in the background, but my ears feel clogged and I'm wrapped in a sound-deadening bubble.

The paramedics carefully make their way to the boy, as crewmembers from other teams slowly winch the sled back toward the track.

As the skis slide out of the deep powder, a single red streak drags across the white.

"Stop!" I wave my hands wildly and grip the arm of one of the mechanics. "Stop the winch. There's blood!" And that's when the knot in my stomach unfurls.

Someone *is* dead . . . but it isn't Trey.

CHAPTER 4

THIS MORNING'S FOG of inexplicable dread now makes perfect sense. You know that scene in the movie when time seems to slow down and the edges of the main character's vision get fuzzy as he or she laser focuses on one pivotal thing? That's exactly what's happening to me right now, and that one pivotal thing is a crimson slash in the otherwise pristine snow.

My stomach swirls, and the burning message from my mood ring must be ignored, as I hoof it up the slope and deposit this morning's breakfast behind a birch tree.

Despite my father's preoccupation with getting Trey safely strapped onto a backboard, he calls out to me. "Mitzy, you okay?"

Picking up a handful of icy flakes, I clean my

mouth before replying. "I'll live." Oh brother! What a poor choice of words.

"Hey, can you push back the crowds? I'm gonna find Trey's parents and his coach."

The word "coach" seems to freeze in the air like a group of floating icicles, and the burning message in my mood ring's black cabochon can no longer be avoided. I yank off my layers of mittens and gaze into the glass dome. The unmistakable face staring back at me nearly brings up another batch of home fries.

Shoving my hand back into the mittens, I jog down the hill and call out to my father. "Dad, I need to talk to you."

He sees the panicked look on my face and pats the paramedic on the back as he struggles back onto the stability of the hard-packed drag track. "What is it?"

I gesture hesitantly toward the site of the accident, but refuse to turn my head. "Under there, the body . . . It's Mr. Jablonski."

The color drains from Jacob's face. "Are you sure? You're positive it's Jawbone?"

Nodding my head slowly, I grip my dad's arm as icy tears form in the corners of my eyes. "You know what that means, right? Stellen's an . . . He's . . . an orphan."

Jacob holds me tight, and for a moment his love

keeps the horrible montage, pressing at the edges of my consciousness, at bay. Stellen may not be eleven, but even at the sort-of-grown-up age of sixteen, losing both your parents in the space of five years is going to leave scars. "I need to get out to his place. I don't want him to hear about this when some deputy shows up on his doorstep."

Jacob nods solemnly. "Somebody needs to clear this area, though."

"Yeah, it's definitely a crime scene. I'll call Erick. You go find Trey's folks. I've got a fan club that will handle crowd control, and then I'm heading out to find Stellen."

"Fan club?" He lifts an eyebrow and shrugs. "I'll be over to check on you tonight."

Drawing a ragged breath, I struggle to hold it together. "Thanks, Dad." I slip my phone out and risk baring a hand to call the sheriff. Erick's friendly voice nearly cracks my fragile exterior. "Hey, it's a long story, and I promise to explain tonight— What? Yes, it's a corpse, but— You can tease me about it later. The victim is Mr. Jablonski, the taxidermist."

"Hey! Hey, no civilians on the drag track. If you're not wearing official race-staff safety gear, you better get off my track. I'll have you arrested—or worse."

An official-looking man in a bright-orange

safety vest with a clipboard in his left hand is running up the hill toward my father and me.

My dad calls out. "Look, pal, I know you think you're in charge, but we have an emergency situation. You're going to have to cancel the races."

The man plants his feet on the track and shakes his head firmly. "I *am* in charge. And you and this girl better get off my track or heads are going to roll. I don't make empty threats."

My father points to the carmine stain in the powder and shakes his head.

I give Erick the two-second update and place him on speakerphone as I aim the device at Mr. Hothead.

A calm, official voice takes control of the situation. "Mr. Bennett, this is Sheriff Harper. You need to shut down the drags and the snocross immediately. No one is to leave the grounds. No additional races are to take place. I have deputies en route to secure the scene and take statements from the eyewitnesses. Do you understand?"

The all-bark-and-no-bite official nods.

I kick out one hip and tilt my head. "You'll have to give a verbal answer for the record, Mr. Bennett."

"Yes, Sheriff. Yes, I understand. I'll take care of it right away." His suddenly cooperative head continues to nod.

"Thank you, Mr. Bennett." Erick swallows and exhales audibly.

I tap the speaker off and press the phone against my beanie. "Don't worry, I'm headed out to break the news to Stellen. I feel so awful for him."

My wonderful boyfriend attempts to console me, but I can't risk it. The tears are too close to the surface. "I gotta go. Dinner at the bookshop? Yeah, I will. Bye."

As I slide the phone into my pocket, a movement on the hill catches my eye. A jester hat bobs up the slopes. "Bristol!"

She sees me and lopes forward with the determination of a hungry lone wolf.

"Bristol, get AJ up here and clear these people out. Find some rope or something and set up a perimeter. This is a crime scene."

She bows clumsily, turns, and shouts down the mountain with shocking volume. "Mitzy Moon is on the case."

I hang back until I see her and AJ headed up the slope, dragging long strands of plastic pennant-flag garland in their wake. All right, they've got this. Now it's time to deliver the worst news any kid could ever receive.

The Jeep seems to drive itself out to the old Jablonski farm. I certainly can't see the road. Tears blur my vision and I allow it to happen now, so I can be strong for Stellen.

Making the final turn by the crumbling silo—excellent landmark—I frown at the bare-limbed trees arching over the road. The grey skies hang heavier, as the road narrows to a single track through the deep snow. This drive has all the makings of a scary movie intro.

The old taxidermy shed looms into view and my skin crawls with the unwelcome thought of what it houses. I park in front of the dark and dreary main cabin, mount the steps and knock on the door.

No reply.

There's no bell, so I try the handle.

The door opens and I push my way inside. "Stellen? Stellen, it's Mitzy Moon. Are you in here?"

No reply.

He could be out visiting his memory meadow, the place where we cemented our friendship over the loss of loving mothers. However, my psychic senses tell me he's in the taxidermy shed. The absolute last place I want to go.

Time to put on my big-girl pants and woman up.

I trudge across the driveway and brush the falling snow from my face. Hopefully, the cold temperatures will shrink the puffiness under my eyes and it won't look like I've been crying for twenty minutes.

The handle turns easily, and I step inside. Before I can call out, my gaze locks onto a pair of black-tufted ears—frozen in time. The horrible sight of a stuffed caracal, eternally leaping in the air to grab a bird, sucker punches me right in the gut. "Pyewacket!" I lunge forward, grab the statue and force myself to look at its face. Is this why he was missing?

Stellen appears between a mound of prepared hides and the naked armature of a mountain lion. "Mitzy? What are you doing here?" He takes in my terrified expression as I clutch the mounted caracal, and he thinks he's solved the mystery. "Oh, that's not . . . It's a really long story. Don't worry, I would never let my wacko dad stuff your cat." He shakes his head and laughs a little.

The mounted cat has no scars over its left eye, and my panic evaporates. But, before I deliver my heartbreaking news, I'll let the kid have this moment. I'll let him have the last laugh he'll have for—possibly years.

He steps forward and helps me right the stuffed wildcat. "My dad's not here. Big snowmobile race at the mountain, you know?"

Taking a deep breath, I struggle to find an

ounce of courage. "That's why I'm here, Stellen. Maybe you should sit down?" In the movies, they always tell people to sit down before bad news. I suppose it's to keep them from injuring themselves when they faint, but nowadays fainting doesn't seem to be nearly as common as it was in the Victorian era.

He shrugs. "I'm fine. What's going on?"

"There was an accident during the drag races, and—"

"Oh no. Did Trey get hurt? If Trey got hurt my dad's gonna be furious. He was counting on his take of the winnings to pay his entry fees into the Taxidermy World Championships."

Despite the horrible news I'm trying to share, the thought of the Taxidermy World Championship momentarily pulls my focus. "There's a world championship?"

Stellen rolls his eyes dramatically. "You don't wanna know. Anyway, is Trey gonna be all right?"

"I don't know for sure. I had to leave. There's more. It's your dad."

The young boy's eyes widen, and his uncanny intuition jumps ahead. He stammers, "My . . . my dad was injured? In the accident?"

This is uncharted territory for me. I can't very well tell the kid that a snowmobile skewered his father's buried body! There's gotta be some of that decorum Silas is always talking about hidden inside me somewhere. I search my brain for the right words.

Stellen lowers himself onto the pile of hides. "It's bad, isn't it?"

"I didn't want you to have to hear it from the sheriff, you know?"

He nods and blinks his watery eyes. "How bad is it?"

"Stellen, I'm afraid your father is dead." I could've used some cheesy euphemism, but it's better to give it to him straight. It's not going to make it hurt any less if I confuse the kid with a "no longer with us" or a "slipped away." At the end of the day, his dad is dead. Nice words won't change that.

His gaze slowly scans from one side of the shop to the other, taking in all the treasures and trophies his father held in such high regard. "What am I gonna do with all of this?"

"You don't need to worry about that. There will be an investigation. I'm sure the sheriff will send a team out to look for evidence—"

The young man jumps to his feet and steps toward me. "Wait, it wasn't an accident? He wasn't killed in the race? You think he was murdered?" His breathing is rapid and shallow.

Placing a hand on his shoulder, I offer the only

comfort I can. "I think he was murdered, and I'm going to find out who did it."

Stellen paces a tight circle and taps his forehead with two fingers on his right hand. "What am I gonna do? Where am I gonna live? Maybe I can petition the court to become an emancipated minor. I don't have any—" He stops and his right hand slowly falls to his side like the lazy flakes outside the window. His eyes glaze over and his jaw hangs slack.

The crippling overwhelm. I know it too well. "I tell you what, let's go inside and pack up a bag or two. I'm sure you have schoolbooks, projects, favorite clothes . . . You can come and stay with me until everything is settled. All right?"

The boy's intelligent green eyes narrow and he tilts his head of dark-brown curls with concern. "I'm not sure Child Protective Services will allow me to stay with someone who's not a relative."

"I hold quite a bit of sway over the sheriff. You let me and him worry about CPS." I slide a friendly arm around his shoulder and intend to guide him into the house.

Instead, he turns into me and weeps. It's all I can do to hold it together and be a rock.

A few moments pass and Stellen turns away to wipe his eyes, too embarrassed to look at me.

"Hey, I was only eleven when I lost my mom. I

cried for a solid week. You never have to feel self-conscious around me. All right? Let's go get your stuff, and you can help me find the real Pyewacket when we get back to the bookshop."

He swipes at his tears and silently leads the way into his empty house.

Stellen pulls a carry-on-sized suitcase from under his bed, unzips it, and places the open clamshell on his bed. As he collects random items from around his room, his inner world pours out of his mouth.

"My dad always wanted me to ride, you know? It's not my thing. I can't play sports, I wasn't into taxidermy, and I don't like snow-mobiles."

He places a stack of books next to the stack of cards, still tucked in envelopes, he'd pulled out of his bedside table. "I guess I was a disappointment to him. He wanted some kind of super manly jock for a son, and I was a nerdy bookworm."

He picks up a picture of his mother from a small desk, shoved into a poorly illuminated corner, and holds the frame as though it could disintegrate in his hands at any moment. "Will I ever be back? Should I take the photo albums from the living room?"

"I'm not going to let anything happen to this place, Stellen. It'll be here as long as you need it to be here. You don't have to worry about making any major decisions today, all right?"

He nods and places the photo of his mom in the suitcase.

I hate to interrupt his process, but the bag is half full, and it doesn't contain any clothing. "You should grab some clothes. Stuff for school, and something nice for the—funeral."

"I have a suit, but I haven't worn it since her— It probably doesn't fit."

"No sweat. We'll take care of that later. Just grab some school clothes, pajamas, and you can bring your pillow if you want."

He sits down on his bed and stares at me with sadness and a hint of apprehension. "I don't have pajamas. I usually sleep in my clothes. My dad never checks on me."

This kid is crushing my heart, piece by piece. "That's all right. Do you have some sweatpants, or something comfortable? I don't mean to freak you out, but there's only one enormous studio apartment at my place. I'll set you up on the sofa, but I'd hate for you to have to sleep in jeans."

For the first time since I offered him a place to stay, Stellen seems to be processing the reality of moving in with me. My regular and psychic senses pick up on an increase in his discomfort.

"Don't worry. You'll have some privacy. We'll

set up a bathroom schedule, and— We'll make it work. You'll get settled in no time. I promise."

He nods and retrieves some items of clothing from the floor of his closet.

Never let it be said that teenage boys are neat freaks. Despite his above-average intelligence and bookworm tendencies, he's still a dyed-in-the-wool slob.

He zips the suitcase and grabs his pillow. "I'll get my winter gear downstairs, and I have to set the alarm on the shop before I leave."

"What about the house?"

"There's nothing in here anyone would want. All the valuable stuff is in the taxi shop."

Turning the lights off in his room as we leave, I follow Stellen down the narrow staircase and try to ignore the hollow emptiness that threatens to swallow us. There's nothing left in this building. Once upon a time, long, long ago, it may have been a home, but I think it's barely been a dwelling since his mother passed.

True to his word, Stellen does not bother to lock the house. He slides his suitcase into the back of my Jeep and jogs over to secure the taxidermy shed.

I jump in the vehicle and get the heater running.

He climbs onto the passenger seat and sits quietly as I maneuver around in a seven-point turn to exit the property without hitting any trees. "I need to make a quick call, is that all right?"

He nods and stares out the window mournfully.

No need to explain to Stellen the reasons why I need to call my attorney and secret alchemical mentor. I'm hoping that my wise teacher will read between the lines and help me navigate this strange situation.

"Hey, Silas, I have a project for you and I need a bit of legal advice."

He harrumphs at my lack of proper etiquette, but makes no objections to my request.

"Unfortunately, Mr. Jablonski was found dead this morning at the snocross event on Fox Mountain. I picked up Stellen Jablonski—you met him once at the bookshop—and I offered him a place to stay until we get things sorted out."

Silas jumps in to warn me of the possible legal ramifications of taking in an under-aged child without proper paperwork.

"I know you can sort out the legal side of it for me, and I'm sure even call in a favor from Erick. But the real reason I called is that I'd like you to protect the property from any potential transfer of ownership. Can you find out if Mr. Jablonski had a will? And, also, file whatever injunctions you need to make sure the property can't be sold until Stellen decides what he'd like to do?"

Silas mumbles something about meddling, but I cut him off. "I know it's a lot, but I'm sure you can handle it. Thanks. I look forward to your update tomorrow." I end the call before he can protest.

Stellen presses his cheek against the cold glass, and I know exactly the swirl of emotions and fears coursing through his body.

There's no need to push him to discuss things he's not ready to explore.

Silence can be healing.

It's enough for him to know that I'm here—for as long as it takes.

My eyes scan the road as my mind drifts off to memories of the days following my mother's death. I can't change the past, but at least I can pay it forward.

CHAPTER 5

As though I've slipped into a scene from *Dune*, I seem to fold space and arrive at the bookshop in the blink of an eye. Stopping the vehicle next to the alleyway door, I gesture to the back of the Jeep. "Why don't you grab your bag and wait here while I park this thing?"

"Okay," he mumbles.

Once he's retrieved his suitcase and safely closed the hatch, I pull the Jeep into the garage and take a deep breath.

Unlocking the side door, we step inside and immediately catch Twiggy's attention.

"Who's the tagalong?" She tilts her head and scrutinizes my sidekick.

"Hey, Stellen, how about you head up that circular staircase over there, and I'll join you after I fill Twiggy in? All right?"

He nods and rolls his bag toward the stairs.

Stepping into the back room, I bring Twiggy up to speed on the horrifying events of the morning.

"You're one heckuva corpse magnet, kid. It was good of you to take in the boy, though. I'll call over to the Elks Lodge and see if I can pick up a cot. He can't sleep on that settee for more than a night or two."

I'd like to explain to her how teenage boys can sleep absolutely anywhere, but I know she's trying to help in the only way she can. "Thanks. That would be great."

Out of nowhere she calls out, "You better hook that up behind you, kid."

Wow! I didn't even hear him unhook the "No Admittance" chain. Maybe I'm not the only one with psychic senses. "Go easy on him, Twiggy."

She runs a hand through her short grey pixie cut and shifts her weight from one biker boot to the other. "He ain't made out of glass, Mitzy. The sooner things return to normal, the better off he'll be."

There may be some truth in what she's saying, but I know from experience that nothing in his life will ever return to normal. My best bet is to change the subject. "Did you hear from Amaryllis? About the wedding?"

Twiggy shoves a hand in the pocket of her dungarees and nods. "Yep. I gave her a list of rules for the venue and vendors approved to work on the premises. We should have everything sorted out in a couple of days." She leans in and whispers conspiratorially, "It sure will make your Grams happy to have the wedding here."

I snicker. "Don't I know it? I better go get Stellen settled. Thanks for everything."

"All in a day's work." She returns to her rolly office chair and I tempt fate by stepping over the chain at the bottom of the stairs. The universe smiles down and allows me to pass without a trace— or a tumble.

Upstairs, in the Rare Books Loft, Stellen stands next to one of the oak tables and waits patiently.

"So, now that you're gonna be staying here, you need to learn a few of the secrets. Why don't you do the honors?" I gesture to the candle sconce on the wall and force a smile. "You just tilt it down."

He wheels his suitcase over, reaches up with his left hand, and pulls.

The bookcase door slides open with a satisfying whoosh. Despite Stellen's horrible morning, he manages to mumble, "Sweet."

Chuckling, I invite him into the apartment and

gesture toward the settee. "I'll get some blankets for you. You can sleep here for now, and Twiggy said she'll get you a cot. Which may or may not be more comfortable."

Grams blasts through the wall from the loft into the apartment and it takes all of my self-control not to shout at her.

"Mitzy? Who's the boy?" She gestures at Stellen, who thankfully has his back turned.

I pinch my lips tightly together and take advantage of her ability to read my thoughts. *This is Stellen Jablonski. His father was murdered, and we found his body at the snowmobile drag races this morning. He's staying here indefinitely, and the last thing he needs right now is to be frightened to death by a ghost. So vanish!*

She crosses her arms over her ample bosom and kicks out her hip. "I was here first. He can't see me or hear me, so it doesn't matter if I'm in here. Besides, I came to let you know that I found Pyewacket in the printing museum."

That's great. We'll debate ghost versus guest rules later. For now, make yourself scarce.

She shakes her translucent head and mumbles loudly. "Well, I never."

I shoot one last thought in her direction as she disapparates. *We both know that's not true!*

Her giggle echoes through the ether.

"Mitzy? Sorry. I don't mean to interrupt your thoughts or whatever you—"

Oops. Looks like Stellen may have been talking to me while I was thought-scolding Grams. "Oh, you're fine. I was running through a mental checklist, you know?"

He nods. "Would it be okay if I walk down to the Piggly Wiggly to grab a few things?"

"Of course. Do you need any money?"

He shoves a hand in the pocket of his jeans and pulls out a few crumpled bills. "No. I think I have enough for bread and peanut butter."

How can I be such a dork! The kid probably hasn't eaten all day. "Hey, why don't I take you to lunch at the diner. I'm actually kinda famished." I'll spare him the explanation involving most of my breakfast being left on the mountain.

A hint of color returns to his face and he almost smiles. "I can pay."

"Look, I don't mean to sound like a snobby rich chick, but as long as you're my ward, let's agree that I can definitely afford to feed you. Got it?"

He nods. "Thanks. I don't know why you're being so nice to me. But it means a lot right now."

"I've been where you are. I'm just doing what I wish someone would've done for me. Now, let's go grab some grub. We can't very well hunt wild bookstore caracal on empty stomachs."

And for a split second, the corners of his mouth turn up.

I did that. And that's everything.

Despite his traumatic morning, Stellen has a gargantuan appetite.

Two perfectly cooked cheeseburgers, surrounded by matching mountains of french fries, and a pair of chocolate malts grace the table before us.

Tally refills our waters and tilts her head in that "poor little lamb" way—I remember it all too clearly from my childhood.

The scrape of the spatula against the grill in the kitchen stops, and I look up as Odell approaches.

"You Stan Jablonski's kid?"

Stellen's mouth is far too full to facilitate a verbal answer, so he nods slowly and wipes his mouth with a thin paper napkin.

The lines around Odell's eyes crinkle as he forces a smile. "Sorry about your dad. He was a good guy, and a great taxidermist."

The rate at which news travels in this quaint town never ceases to amaze.

My new roommate swallows roughly and takes a quick sip of his water. "Thanks. You know— knew my dad?"

"Indirectly. My brother Walt, God rest him, used to run the Walleye Lodge out on Fish Hawk Island."

Stellen nods knowingly. "Oh, yeah. My dad did a lot of quick turnaround fish mounting for that guy. He ran charter boats, too, right?"

Odell nods appreciatively. "Smart kid. You two oughta get along great."

I blush a little at the compliment, but smile with gratitude.

My surrogate grandfather puts one hand on our table and leans down as he gestures toward me with his thumb. "I got this one on the free burgers and fries for life plan. I'm happy to offer you the same deal whenever you're in town."

Stellen's face kind of freezes, and my psychic senses feel his emotions swirling too close to the surface.

Time for me to jump in and create a distraction. "You might regret that, Odell. Stellen is bunking with me until Silas gets everything sorted out with Mr. Jablonski's will."

Odell stands up and chuckles. "Well, it's too late now. A deal's a deal." He raps his knuckles twice on the silver-flecked white Formica table and returns to the kitchen.

Stellen blinks rapidly and avoids my gaze.

"You ready to head back to the store and look for that wildcat?"

He grabs his napkin, and, as he pretends to wipe his mouth, swipes at each of his eyes. "Yeah. Sounds good."

I stack our plates, and, before I can say a word, he picks up both of our empty malt cups and follows me to the dish bin behind the counter. He definitely has more than the average teenager's intuition, and manners to boot. I might enjoy having a roomie.

We make slow progress down Main Street, and Stellen clears his throat two or three times. Even someone without the benefit of psychic senses could tell he needs to say something.

"Just a reminder, you can tell me anything you want any time. No judgment. I promise."

He exhales, and I can sense his relief. "I really appreciate everything you're doing for me, and I don't want to sound ungrateful, or whatever."

"You won't. What do you need?"

"I don't know the bus schedules around here. So, I'm not sure how I'm gonna get to school on Monday."

Wow! I can't believe he's thinking about school. That would've been the last thing on my mind at his age. In fact, at his age, I was deep into the undesirable crowd, skipping school, shoplifting, and practicing my lock-picking skills whenever I could. Maybe I should be *his* ward. "Are you sure you're ready to go to school on Monday?"

"No. But I'm sure I don't wanna sit around all day and think about what might've happened to my dad."

"All right. You let me know how you're feeling Monday morning. If you want to go to school, I'll drive you to school. If you want to stay home, I'll have Silas take care of everything."

We take a few more steps before Stellen asks another question. "So, um, Silas Willoughby is your attorney, right? He does a lot of stuff for you. It almost seems like he's family."

Now it's my turn to uncomfortably blink back tears. "I guess he's a little bit of both. He started out as my attorney, but over the last year or so he's definitely taken a more important role in my life." There, that's truthful and yet vague enough to keep all our collective secrets.

We cross First Avenue and I retrieve the hefty, one-of-a-kind brass key that opens my special front door.

Stellen runs his fingers over the carvings and mumbles little phrases out loud as he traces the characters. "Chiron and Hippodamia. Pan and the gift of Aphrodite." When his hand reaches the carving of the wildcat, he crouches and leans his face close to the timber. "This looks like a caracal."

I have to chuckle. "It definitely does."

His touch moves over the cat's face. "Looks like he was injured."

"Again, I'd have to agree."

A frosty gust of wind curls around the corner of the building from the harbor, and my teeth chatter. "Not to rush you, but do you mind if we continue this discussion inside?"

His eyes snap up, as though he's only just realized he wasn't alone. "Yeah. Sure. Sorry."

We walk into the bookstore, throw our heavy coats over the "No Admittance" chain, and I lead the way into the printing museum.

"Is that a real Gutenberg press?"

I give a low whistle and nod. "Impressive guess. What do you think you know about ancient printing technology?"

He proceeds to download more information than I ever wanted to hear on the topic.

My eyes widen with each additional fact. "That'll do, *Wikipedia*."

His cheeks flush self-consciously and he kicks the toe of his shoe at an invisible rock. "I read a lot of books and watch way too many YouTube videos."

"I didn't have a lot of friends growing up ei-

ther." Giving his back a friendly pat, I continue toward the stairs. "Now let's find that cat."

As we approach the landing, I call out. "Pye?
Pyewacket, I have someone to introduce to you."

We complete our search of the second floor and
come up empty-pawed. When we're about to walk
into the third-floor exhibits, I send a quick mental
message to Grams. *Please don't scare the boy. We're
just trying to find Pyewacket.*

As we turn the corner, I see the drawers open
on the antique writing desk, and the stack of papers
representing Ghost-ma's memoirs has nearly dou-
bled since my last visit to her writing alcove.

Next to the stack of papers, Pyewacket is
stretched lazily over the top of the desk, feigning a
deep sleep. Unfortunately, the ghost of Myrtle
Isadora is seated at her writing desk, with one shimmering limb scratching between Pyewacket's tufted
ears and the other busily writing with a quill pen.

The next irreversible sequence of events occurs
almost simultaneously.

Pyewacket growls.

Grams drops her quill pen and flickers out of
sight.

Stellen gasps and stops moving, but instead of
screaming with fright, his eyes sparkle with hope.

I hustle in to erase the obvious. "Well, there's
Pyewacket. Let's head back to the apartment and

make some microwave popcorn." And the award for lamest distractionary technique goes to . . .

"Was that a ghost? Is this museum haunted? That's so lit!"

Forcing a dismissive chuckle, I stride toward Pyewacket and make up a story as I go. "Oh, I think Pyewacket was just playing with some of the props. You know how cats are with feathers." I whisper to Pye, "Help me out, buddy. We gotta get the kid back to the apartment."

Pyewacket stretches his glorious tan form, leaps off the desk, and races down the stairs.

"Let's head out." I gesture like a children's television host trying to make room cleanup sound fun.

Stellen's momentary spark of life drifts away and his eyes glaze over. "I guess you don't believe in ghosts, huh?"

When in doubt, lie it out. "I don't know. I never really thought about it. Why?"

"Never mind. It's stupid." He shuffles down the stairs.

"It's not stupid." I toss some encouragement over my shoulder as we cross the main floor. "Say whatever you want."

He follows me silently into the apartment and I motion for him to sit on the sofa.

He chews on a fingernail and casually wipes a little tear from the corner of his eye. "My mom's ghost used to visit me sometimes. Like when I was sick, or after my dad would yell at me. I'd go up to my room and just sit in the dark and wish that she was still alive, you know?"

"Yeah. I know exactly what you mean." Raw emotions scratch at my heart. "Did you actually see her?"

"I don't know, maybe. Never mind, it makes me sound crazy." He looks away.

"It doesn't make you sound crazy. What I meant was, was it a feeling? Like, did you feel her spirit in the room, or did you actually see her ghost?"

Stellen crosses his arms over his chest and curves forward. "Promise not to laugh?"

"Absolutely. It helps to talk about it. Honestly." As I sit in the scalloped-back chair, normally reserved for my mentor Silas, it feels strange to be the one asking the difficult questions, rather than struggling to answer them.

Stellen rocks almost imperceptibly, and his voice is faint and uncertain. "She looked like before —before she was sick. She was wearing that dumb dress that my dad gave to the funeral home. She wanted to be buried in her favorite jeans and a sweatshirt I gave her for her last Mother's Day." He sniffles. "My dad said it was undignified."

"What did the sweatshirt say?"

A wry grin tugs at the corners of his mouth. "Secretly hoping CHEMO will give me SU-PERPOWERS."

My heart aches for this grieving boy, but the shirt is mad snarky. "Sounds like your mom had a great sense of humor."

"She really did. Right up until the end, you know?"

"I wish I could've met her."

He nods and swallows loudly.

"How many times did you see her ghost?"

"Quite a few. I kind of lost track. I started to take it for granted." He looks at me and bites hard on his fingernail. "What if she can't find me here?"

I have no idea how to answer that, but his story sounds too believable and my concern for the area of impact widens. "Have you seen other ghosts? I mean, besides your mom?"

Stellen's crossed arms remain tight against his body, but his spine straightens. "Mostly animals. That's why I hated my dad's shop."

Leaning against the chair, I exhale and let my head fall back. Staring at the ceiling, I'm at a complete loss for words.

"Do you believe me?" His tone borders on desperation.

I bend forward and place an elbow on each of

my knees as I gaze directly into his worried green eyes. "I do. I do believe you."

He sighs, gulps in air, and leans back.

My psychic senses uncover a flood of relief rushing through him.

Before I have a chance to recap or throw him one of my amazing conversation starters, Twiggy's voice blares over the intercom. "Sheriff Harper's here. Want me to send him up?"

Stellen jumps and a measure of his earlier unease returns. "Do you want me to leave? Or wait outside?"

"What? Why would I want you to leave?"

"Well, I thought you guys were, like, hooking up."

An unexpected surge of laughter grips me, and I cover my mouth with one hand as I nod. "Um, we are *dating*. But I'm pretty sure he's here on business."

Stellen's face falls. "Oh, about my dad?"

His half question, half statement hangs in the air as I walk to the intercom and reach for the button. "Yeah, send him up." Turning to Stellen, I offer the only reassurance I have. "I'll handle this, all right? Let me do the talking."

He nods, but his energy is giving off a decidedly "freaked" vibe.

CHAPTER 6

PRESSING THE TWISTING ivy ridges on the plaster medallion, I paste on a smile as the bookcase slides open.

Erick walks across the mezzanine in his perfectly pressed tan uniform with his dark-brown winter jacket draped over his left arm, and my heart speeds up a few beats per minute. His eyes catch the light and he flashes a crooked grin.

My brain is telling me he's here on business and it's a standard-issue uniform, but that man could make a burlap sack look sexy!

"Hey, Moon. We need to talk about your kidnapping."

My eyes widen. "I wasn't kidnapped. Obviously, I'm standing right here. Clearly not abducted." I gesture magnanimously toward my person.

He walks into my apartment, tilts his head toward the minor posted up on my settee, and scrunches up his face.

"Oh, that kidnapping." My confident gaze falters. "He wasn't coerced. He needed a place to stay." A sudden angle pops into my head and bolsters my courage. "He's my ward."

"Look, Moon, you're not Bruce Wayne. There are rules for a reason. Minors can't give consent."

My clairsentience picks up on an instant heightening of fear, and Stellen jumps to my rescue.

"Mitzy is just letting me stay here until everything gets sorted out with my dad. She fed me lunch and she's gonna take me to school on Monday, and everything."

Erick's features soften and he smiles wistfully. "I wish it was that easy, Stellen. But—" His cell phone interrupts the lecture. "It's the station. I gotta take this." Erick steps back into the Rare Books Loft and Stellen fidgets nervously.

Gesturing toward the boy, I wave my hand in a "simmer down" motion. "Don't worry. You're not leaving this apartment. I still have a few tricks up my sleeve."

Stellen gnaws on another fingernail.

Erick slips his phone into his pocket. A frustrated, but unsurprised, grin spreads across his face as he returns. "You really are something else."

"Thank you for noticing." I take a bow. "Can you be more specific?"

"That was Silas Willoughby on the phone. They patched him through from the station. Apparently he's representing the minor Jablonski and has arranged for Mizithra Moon to take temporary custody."

I look over my shoulder at Stellen and wink. "See, all legal and above board, Sheriff."

Erick offers me a tantalizing smile and my tummy flip-flops as I forge ahead. "So, did you just come to arrest me for kidnapping, or is there more to this house call?"

"I need to ask him some questions. Stellen, do you want your attorney present?"

Stepping forward, I place a firm hand on Erick's arm. "You don't think for one minute that—"

"Easy, Batgirl. I need to get some background information, and anything suspicious he may have noticed in the last week or so. He's not a suspect."

Stellen nods nervously. "It's okay. You can ask me whatever you want."

"Thanks." Erick turns to me and hits me with his irresistible puppy-dog eyes. "Can I trouble you for a cup of coffee, Miss Moon?"

"No trouble at all. It'll only take a sec." I hurry to the back room and bump into Pyewacket on the circular stairs.

Crouching down, I whisper a quiet warning to the fiendish feline. "I know you don't like guests, but Stellen lost his dad, and he's all alone in the world. We're gonna take care of him until Silas works things out. All right?"

"Reow." Can confirm.

"Oh, and I'm fairly certain he can see ghosts. So play it cool, and help me keep Grams out of the apartment."

Pyewacket tilts his head, narrows his eyes, and replies, "Ree-oow." Conspiratorial agreement.

By the time I return with two mugs of coffee and a can of pop, Erick is seated across from Stellen and has his notepad and pen in hand. I set a mug on the coffee table in front of Erick, pass the soda to Stellen, and take a seat next to him on the settee.

Sheriff Harper hits him with the standard barrage of questions about rival coaches, unhappy snowmobile students, and wonders if Stellen ever overheard his dad arguing with Trey Lee or his parents.

"I'm really sorry I can't be more help, Sheriff. I'm not into snowmobiles, you know? That part of my dad's life was totally separate. He hated that I didn't ride. It was one of the things him and my mom argued about the most."

Erick puts away his pad and pen, picks up his coffee, and leans back in the chair. "Thanks for your help. I know it's hard to talk about. We should have the medical examiner's report in a day or two, and once we establish time of death I might have a few more questions for you. I hope that's okay?"

"Yeah. It's fine."

An awkward silence falls between us.

Sheriff Harper manages a bumpy topic shift. "Hey, you guys mind if I order some pizzas? The investigation ran through lunch and I'm so hungry I could eat my own boot."

Stellen gives me a sideways glance, and I easily interpret his response.

"I think that sounds great. What's your favorite topping, buddy?"

The boy shrugs. "Whatever you guys like. I'll pretty much eat anything."

Erick leans forward. "Let's say it's your birthday, and money is no object. What kind of pizza would you order?"

Stellen chews his bottom lip and stammers. "Is it— Do I have to— Can it be more than one thing?"

The sheriff gives a friendly laugh and nods. "There's no limit. You want all the toppings on one pizza? You got it. You want just pineapple and nothing else? You got it. Come on, what's your dream pizza?"

For the first time since I picked Stellen up from his house, I sense a shift in his energy. For a moment, he's actually forgotten he's an orphan. Bless Sheriff Harper's little heart.

"Okay, this is going to sound weird, but I would get pepperoni, bacon, jalapeños, onions, and pineapple."

Erick slaps his hand on his thigh. "Now that's what I'm talking about. That's a pizza. What about you, Moon? You got a favorite?"

"I'm feeling like barbecued chicken with green onions and extra cheese? Can you guys handle that?"

My amazing boyfriend pulls out his phone and apparently has a pizza place on speed dial. He tips the phone away from his lips and whispers, "Do you have more soda, or should I order some?"

"I've got plenty of pop." It still gives me a little giggle to use the local colloquialism for soft drinks.

He nods, and his voice is all business as he places the order for our two outrageous pizzas, plus a large Italian sausage.

Rubbing my hands together to create the appearance of anticipation, I attempt to lighten the mood. "You guys wanna play a board game or something while we wait for the 'Za'?"

Stellen smiles, an actual almost-cheerful smile. "Is it lame if I say Scrabble?"

As if on cue, Pyewacket struts into the room,

plops down at the end of the coffee table and fixes our new guest with a golden-eyed stare.

"Funny you should mention Scrabble. My grandmother literally won ol' Pyewacket here while betting in an off-the-books Scrabble game. But you didn't hear that from me, Sheriff."

Erick unbuttons his collar and comically places a hand over his badge. "Let's drop the formalities. We're just hanging out, getting to know each other. Keeping it casual. No titles. Sound good?"

Stellen nods. "Sure. Sweet."

I wink. "Whatever you say, *Ricky*."

Sheriff Too-Hot-To-Handle blushes a delightful shade of crimson when I use his mother's nickname for him.

I fetch the Scrabble game and the play quickly shifts from friendly to intense. I always knew Erick was above average, but his skill with the tiles is impressive. Oh, and let's not forget little Stellen! The kid has a shockingly advanced vocabulary. Some of the medical terms and names of bones he's throwing onto the board would be awe-inspiring coming from a neurosurgeon.

BING. BONG. BING.

Erick jumps up. "I'll get the door. Don't look at my tiles while I'm gone."

I giggle and cover my mouth with one hand.

As he walks out of the apartment he says, "Yeah, I was talking to you, Moon."

"Where did you learn all of this medical terminology?"

Stellen takes a deep breath and rubs both palms on his jeans. "I have to help my dad. I hate it in the taxi shed, but he gets really busy, and it's—it was—our only income, besides coaching."

"So what does helping your dad stuff animals for hunters have to do with your vocabulary?"

I can almost see the light bulb flick on in his head. "Oh that. The basis of any good taxidermy is anatomy. I didn't like mounting the pieces, but I used all the knowledge of anatomy and stuff to help prepare me for college, you know?"

"What do you want to study?"

"I want to be a veterinarian. Maybe I can make up for all the money my dad made dealing in death by saving a few animals' lives."

"That's an awesome idea." And suddenly a light bulb clicks on in my own head. "Hey, could you handle a *new* after-school job?"

"Do you think I should finish the orders that my dad was working on?"

Rubbing my chin for a moment, I struggle with the question. In the end, I offer Stellen the permission he needs to quit the family business. "Anyone who had an order in with your dad will understand that it's not going to get completed. Maybe you can help Silas sort through all the pending ones and he can contact people to pick up their projects—as is. I don't want you to have to stuff another dead thing as long as you live."

He breathes an enormous sigh of relief. "Thanks. So, what kind of after-school job? Like bagging groceries at the Piggly Wiggly?"

"Nope. What would you say to being an apprentice to Doc Ledo at the Pin Cherry Animal Hospital?"

Stellen's eyes widen with disbelief. "Are you messing with me?"

Erick returns with the pizzas, just in time to jump on the bandwagon. "If she said something that's too good to be true, let me be the first to break it to you, it's true. She's got an uncanny thing with hunches." He places one pizza on the coffee table and two on the floor. "I hope you guys don't mind this buffet arrangement?"

Stellen leans forward and exhales with force. "Are you serious? You could actually get me a job with Doc Ledo?"

"Of course. But, if you want to get into veterinary medicine, your grades are going to have to be way above average. How many hours a week can you work and still keep your academic record in tiptop shape?"

Stellen smiles and there's a positive tone in his voice that surprises me. "As many hours as he wants. I'm so far ahead, at school. I've been doing extra projects, and even some independent study. I can totally work every day. Even weekends. Whatever he needs."

Erick chuckles and wipes some tomato sauce from the corner of his mouth. "I wish I had a couple deputies with that much energy."

"I'll call the doc tomorrow and set everything up. For now, let's dig into our amazing creations."

Stellen nods eagerly. "Yeah, I'm starved." He grabs a paper plate and loads it up with half a pizza.

Everything is going swimmingly and the guys are taking turns throwing meat projectiles in the air for Pyewacket to retrieve.

My fur baby does not disappoint. He leaps with deadly grace and never misses his target.

One more Scrabble game turns into three and the pizza eventually disappears. At the end of the evening, Stellen is the big winner, but refuses to take any credit. "I just got good tiles, you know? Luck of the draw."

Erick chuckles. "Come on, man. Take the win. You definitely earned it."

Nodding, I wipe a streak of pizza sauce from my chin. "Yeah, clearing your board not once, but twice, and hitting three triple word scores is a little bit more than the luck of the draw."

He shrugs. "Okay. I guess I played pretty good."

Sheriff Harper stands and retrieves his jacket. "There's no 'pretty good' about it. You crushed us."

The young man allows himself a smile, but continues to stare at the floor.

"Moon, I'll let you know if the ME's report comes in tomorrow." Erick heads for the door, and I jump up to follow.

"I'll be back in a minute, Stellen. I need to set the alarm after Erick leaves."

Stellen looks up at me and smirks. "Sure. Whatever you say."

"Mind your own business, kid." I toss him a playful glare. It's none of his business if I plan to sneak in a goodbye kiss before I set the aforementioned alarm.

He turns, folds the board, and dumps the tiles into the bag.

At least we gave him a few hours' reprieve from the day's tragedy.

"Wait up, Sheriff. I'll walk you out."

Erick pauses at the top of the spiral staircase and glances over his shoulder. "For a minute there, I thought I might have to beg."

Shoving him gently, I snicker and hurry downstairs.

Under the crimson glow of the EXIT sign, he slips his arms around my waist and pulls me close. "You're lucky that you have Silas to cover your tracks. Next time, try filling me in on your hare-brained schemes. I know people at CPS too. I could've gotten the temporary custody order for you. Remember, I'm on your side—most of the time."

Before he can offer any additional lectures, warnings, or admonitions, I push up on my tiptoes and plant a kiss on his full lips. "Copy that."

He tips his head and departs out the side door. "See ya tomorrow, Moon."

"You absolutely will."

CHAPTER 7

MORNING DAWNS without ceremony and I take the first bathroom time slot. I gesture silently to Stellen when I exit the facilities, and he takes his turn. We bundle in our winter gear and trudge down the street to the diner. Neither of us has the energy to navigate the checkerboard of shoveled and un-shoveled sections of the sidewalk. Instead, we keep our boots low and kick a path straight to breakfast.

Odell gives us a greeting, and as we slide into a booth Tally sets down a steaming cup of coffee and a luscious mug of hot chocolate with whipped cream.

"Morning, Mitzy, and guest."

"Good morning, Tally. Looks like you're playing favorites already." I gesture to the cocoa.

"You know me, I've got a soft spot for kids."

She turns to leave, and I suddenly remember one of my promises. "Oh, Tally, do you have a minute?"

"For you? Always."

"Stellen here is a whiz with anatomy, and he's planning to go to veterinary school after graduation. Do you think—?"

"Glory be! You must be psychic or something, sweetie. Ledo called me just last night to say that one of his vet techs had to go out on maternity leave. He sure could use an extra set of hands—as soon as possible."

Stellen looks at me and shakes his head in disbelief. "There's something about you . . . How can I ever make it up to you?"

Tally answers for me. "Pshaw! You don't owe anybody anything. Mitzy only wants what's best for you, and you'll be helping out my brother, not the other way around. Can I tell him you'll start tomorrow?"

I raise my hand and attempt to buy Stellen some time. "Tomorrow is a little soon. Let's say he'll start Wednesday. We have a few things to work out. I'm sure you understand."

"You betcha. I'll let Ledo know he can expect a new apprentice on Wednesday." She smiles at

Stellen. "You know, if you take the bus that runs through The Pines, you can jump off on Gunnison before it makes that last turn and it'll take you right to the clinic."

I see a cloud pass over Stellen's eyes, and I jump to his rescue. "I'll take him over and make the introductions. I'd love to see the doc and check out the modifications he's made at the clinic."

Tally nods, and her scarlet-red bun bobs up and down. "Sounds good."

As she ducks behind the counter to grab the coffeepot, Odell approaches with our breakfasts.

I know I'll be getting what I want, but I can't wait to see what he thinks Stellen might have wanted.

He pushes a plate in front of me, and I smile with satisfaction. As he sets the second plate down in front of Stellen, I watch the boy's eyes widen with surprise and a hint of trepidation. "How did you—?"

Odell fixes the boy with a kind gaze. "I usually have a pretty good idea what folks need. Enjoy." He raps the table twice and disappears into the kitchen.

Stellen picks up a fork and pauses as he admires his breakfast. "I haven't had french toast since my mom died. It's my absolute favorite."

My mouth is already stuffed full of delicious home fries, so I nod and smile. Once we finish our breakfasts, which doesn't take long, we walk back to the bookstore where Twiggy is unboxing a recent shipment of rare books from Eastern Europe.

"Hey, kid."

Both Stellen and I answer the call.

Twiggy cackles mercilessly and gestures to Stellen. "I was talking to the new recruit. Can you spare him for an hour or so? I could use some help cataloging this shipment."

"I don't really have anything else planned for us. I need to head over to the station later and check on the reports. Until then, you're free to do as you please."

He nods. "I'm happy to help. They look like rad books."

Twiggy chuckles. "Yeah, they're super rad, kid."

"I'll leave you two to handle this, and I'll—"

"I told you she'd be here, man."

"Yeah, not a big stretch, Bristol. She, like, owns the place." Crank shakes his head.

Blerg. Looks like my fan club found my lair. "I'll handle this, Twiggy."

She crosses her arms and a sly grin spreads across her face as though she's swallowed the Cheshire cat. "I'm definitely not gonna miss this."

With a heavy sigh, I step toward the advancing trio. "How can I help you?"

Bristol removes her jester-style stocking cap.

"We heard some stuff on the mountain. We thought you should know. You know, for your investigation."

Twiggy lets out a low whistle behind me. "I didn't realize you were starting a club, doll." She cackles and elbows Stellen playfully.

Stifling my snark, I herd the gang into the children's section under the mezzanine, hopefully out of earshot of my volunteer employee. "Sure, what did you guys hear?"

AJ is the first to share his intel. "So, that organizer guy, Mr. Bennett, that went all aggro on you and your dad, some redhead said she overheard him arguing with Jawbone Friday during the qualifiers."

"Did she say what they were arguing about?"

"Um, no. Like, she couldn't hear what they were saying, just that they both looked angry and the organizer guy shoved Jawbone."

"That could come in handy. Was there anything else?"

Crank takes the next at-bat. "There was some scuttlebutt in the pits. Sounds like Jawbone was gonna take on another student. Priest. His mechanic said Jawbone was inspecting their sled on Friday."

"I thought Mr. Jablonski only coached one student at a time. What changed? And is 'priest' a name or a profession?"

Crank nods furiously. "Totally. You're totally right. But he was gonna cut Trey loose and coach Freddy Priest, the number four seed. Trey's dad was *not* happy. He thought maybe Jawbone was, like, squeezing them for more money, you know?"

"That definitely sounds like motive." I rub my chin and wait for a psychic hit.

Bristol smacks Crank firmly on the back. "See, dude, I told you that was major. Follow the money, right?" Her big brown eyes hold far too much adoration.

"Absolutely. This is great stuff, guys. Thanks for taking the time to come and see me."

No one moves.

"Was there something else?"

Bristol swallows and shifts her weight.

"What is it? Even the smallest details can help, Bristol. Did you hear another argument?"

"No. I just thought it was weird that Jawbone was wearing a helmet—when they pulled the body out, I mean. What would he be doin' out on the mountain with a helmet and no sled?"

"Excellent observation. Seriously, this has been a huge help. I've got to get back to—"

"You gotta set up the murder wall, right?" Bristol nods and grins with anticipation.

If she were a puppy, her tail would be wagging

hard enough to clear a coffee table. "I do. I'll put all this information on there. Again, thanks."

"Cool."

"Sweet."

"Awesome, man."

I show the acolytes to the door and thank them one more time for the information. Attempting to sneak upstairs before Twiggy can take another crack at me meets with epic failure.

"Looks like you got yourself a fan club. How does it feel, doll?"

"It's nice to be appreciated." I step over the chain and march up the stairs in a huff.

Once I'm safely inside the apartment, and the bookcase has whooshed closed behind me, I have to laugh. I never would've imagined a fan club, but I'm not going to look a gift horse in the mouth. They brought me some good leads. "Time to set up the murder wall."

I pause for the interruption that doesn't appear.

Grams must be working on her memoirs. It's not like her to miss interfering with the murder board set up. In her absence, I carefully write out all the cards myself. The rivalries within the snowmobile world sound awfully intense. I wonder how much of this information Erick's deputies gleaned yesterday? Maybe I'll walk down to the station. I need to check on the medical examiner's report, anyway.

The crisp blue sky hugging the harbor belies the sub-zero temps. I turn up my collar against the icy winds, and hustle down the block.

Deputy Baird, or, as I like to call her, Furious Monkeys, after her favorite phone app, gives me a head nod, and I push through the crooked wooden gate into the bullpen. The normally empty desks are crowded with deputies, and typewriter keys are clacking madly. Slipping through the chaos, I peek into Erick's office. "What's going on out there?"

He looks up from a large stack of files on his desk.

"We've gotten over one hundred and fifty tips since yesterday. These guys are working overtime, trying to separate actual leads from dead ends. Not to mention, we've received about thirty calls from the race organizer, demanding to know when he'll be allowed back onto the mountain. Apparently there's another race in the series in two weeks and they need to gather their equipment. So, I brought in some extra guys, and even pulled a few deputies from Broken Rock to help move things along.

"Anything I can do?"

"Sure. You can keep your nose out of this and leave the investigation to the professionals. But saying that out loud feels like throwing an extra gallon of water over Niagara Falls."

An easy laugh escapes. "You're not wrong. I have some information to share. It could be helpful."

"And what do you want in exchange?"

"Just a teensy weensy peek at the medical examiner's report."

He flashes a devious smile. "Let's see how generous you're feeling, Moon. I don't have the report yet, but if you pay it forward, I'll let you sneak that peek tomorrow."

"Deal."

I take a seat on one of the scarred wooden chairs, specifically designed to keep visitors from getting too comfortable, and spill the intel I received from the *Scooby Gang*.

Erick taps his pen on the desk. "I definitely have my opinions about that Bennett character. He's a genuine piece of work. I'll bring him in, but I have a feeling he's more of a typical blowhard than a murderer. However, I'm not ruling anything out."

"What about Trey Lee's dad?"

"That is news. Who did you say your source was?"

"I didn't."

He leans back and crosses his arms behind his head.

Unable to resist, my eyes dart downward, on the off chance that his shirt comes untucked and I get a sneak peek at something better than a medical examiner's report. Although the memory of his abs is never far from my mind, an occasional first-hand account doesn't hurt either.

"Moon? Did I lose you?" His smirk is far too tantalizing.

"I don't know what you mean." The pinkish hue on my traitorous cheeks is all he needs to see.

"Hey, how about I bring some Chinese food over for you and Stellen tonight?"

"Tonight?"

"Yeah. We can watch a couple movies, eat some popcorn, you know . . ."

"I don't think there's going to be any, *you know*, while I have a houseguest, Sheriff."

And now he gets to blush. "Hey, you know what I meant."

"Do I?"

He refuses to take the bait. "Am I bringing the Chinese food or not?"

"Sure. I think Stellen really enjoys hanging out with you. If you bring any movies, though, they have to be VHS tapes."

Erick gasps and leans forward. "Did you say V-H-S?"

"Yep. Grams likes to— liked to keep it old-school."

His gaze narrows. "There's something going on, isn't there, Moon?"

"See you tonight. I've got plenty of microwave popcorn." As I beat a hasty retreat, I hear Erick shout a thank you from his office.

Upon my return to the bookshop, I'm shocked to see the progress Twiggy and Stellen have made on the shipment.

"I'm going to be sorry to see you head off to work for Doc Ledo. You're handy to have around."

Stellen smiles wistfully. "It helps to keep busy."

"It absolutely does. Also, Erick plans to stop over tonight with Chinese food and movies. Sound good?"

He pauses with a large leather tome in hand. "Does he need to ask me more questions?"

"Nope. Nothing official, just to hang out."

"Sweet."

The mood ring on my left hand burns with a message, and when I glance down, I'm surprised to see the face of Silas Willoughby staring back at me. This can't be a coincidence. "What's that book you're holding?"

Stellen glances at the ancient manuscript and shrugs. "My Latin is mostly genus species stuff. Otherwise it's not that good."

A scoff and a chuckle escape before I quip, "It's gotta be better than mine, which is nonexistent." As I walk toward the book, the hairs on the back of my neck tingle. "Hey, Twiggy, we need your help out here."

She stomps out of the back room and fixes me with an impatient stare. "Open the box. Take the book out of the box. Check off the title on the packing list. Seems simple enough to me."

"What's the story behind this one?" I point to the book in Stellen's gloved hands.

Stepping forward to get a better look, she emits a tiny squeak. Twiggy grabs a pair of gloves, slips them on, and snatches the book from his hands. "This is for Willoughby. I'll take care of it."

Stellen looks at me and shrugs.

"Don't worry, you didn't do anything wrong. You keep unpacking boxes, and I'll check back with you later."

Traipsing into the back room, I plunk myself onto a chair. "What's the story with the book?"

Twiggy places the tome into a protective bag, seals it, and slowly turns toward me. "As far as I know, there's only one copy of that thing in the entire world. Willoughby asked me to track it down. He gets first crack at it, and then it's added to the inventory in the loft. Research purposes only. By appointment only."

"Sounds expensive? How much did we pay for it?"

She tilts her head and grins. "Don't worry, Princess, I didn't empty the coffers. Willoughby has this place on a tight budget. He went fifty-fifty on this one."

"Can you read Latin?"

She shrugs. "I've picked up a few things over the years."

"What's it say on the cover?"

Turning toward the book, she gazes through the protective archival sheath and reads aloud. "*Loca Sine Lumine, Loca Sine Lege.*" She chews the inside of her cheek and hums. "It's something about places without light or laws. You'll have to check with Willoughby."

"That sounds sketchy. What's Silas up to?"

She chuckles and shakes her head. "I learned a long time ago not to ask that question, doll."

The burning message from my ring and the tingling in my spine push me to delve deeper into *el misterio del libro*. Yeah, not big on Latin, but I know a little *Español*.

BING. BONG. BING.

"Are you expecting anyone?"

Twiggy shakes her head and spins back to the computer.

It's too early for Erick, so I inch open the side door. "Can I help you?"

The sweet face of Amaryllis peeks through the crack. "I don't have an appointment, but I was hoping you'd have time to go over some wedding stuff. Any chance?"

Pushing the door open wider, I welcome her inside. "Of course. This is the perfect time. Did you want to go to the apartment?"

She rolls her head from side to side. "Well, I wanted to walk around and get a feel for the place. I need to decide where to put guests, where to have the ceremony . . . You know, all the mundane stuff. Maybe you can help?"

"I'd love to. Let's go up to the mezzanine. I think it's the best view, and will give you a better idea what we have to work with. I'm sure we can move—"

"Nope. Nothing gets moved. Check the rules." Twiggy's disembodied voice echoes from the back room as she references the non-negotiable instructions.

Amaryllis and I exchange a silent giggle and hurry up the circular staircase.

"About how many people have you invited?"

She taps her pearlescent fingernail on her lip and hems and haws. "Your dad wanted to keep it extremely small, but it's my first wedding, so I leaned toward more of a spectacle."

"You never married?"

She rolls her eyes. "I know. I know. The truth is, law school consumed me and I started working for Cal Duncan right after graduation. He opened so many doors for me—it was astounding. He had a team of lawyers, and I learned more in those first few years as a junior attorney than in all my time at law school. I sort of lost myself in the work, and barely even dated."

"Well, I want you to have everything exactly as you imagine it. So if—" I lower my voice, lean toward her, and whisper "—we need to move things, I'll make it happen."

She smiles and puts her hand on my shoulder. "Thank you. And thank you for welcoming me into your family. I know you only met your dad last year, and it must be difficult to think about sharing him so soon, but I promise there will always be more than enough room in our lives for you. Any time. I swear."

The urge to hug her overrides my natural tendency to stuff my emotions. "Thank you. I'm looking forward to all of it. The wedding, the extended family, everything."

She chuckles and shakes her head. "You might

want to hold off on saying that until *after* you've met my parents."

My eyes widen. "Anything I should know?"

She leans toward me and whispers, "They definitely don't need to know about my otherworldly mother-in-law."

I clap a hand over my mouth and nod. "Good to know."

We while away the rest of the afternoon planning where guests will sit, who will monitor the guest book, and how we can transform my dusty old bookstore into a sparkling fairytale wedding. When we finish making our lists and sketches, we head back downstairs, just as Stellen is coming up.

"Oh, Amaryllis, this is my houseguest, Stellen Jablonski."

The name sends a flash of recognition across her face. "I'm so sorry for your loss, Stellen. It's nice to meet you, and let us know if there's anything we can do. Jacob and I are just across the alley."

He nods self-consciously and looks down at his feet. "Thanks. Mitzy's helped a lot."

Amaryllis smiles and pats me on the back. "She's rather amazing. I'm sure she'll see that you're well taken care of. Do you have relatives coming to pick you up?"

He shakes his head. "My dad was an only child,

and my mom—" His voice catches in his throat and I jump in.

"I'm going to walk Amaryllis home. The apartment is all yours. If you need anything, let me know." I grip my almost-stepmom by the elbow and tug her down the stairs. As we say our goodbyes, she lowers her voice. "He really doesn't have anyone?"

"I don't know the total story, but Silas told me the family angle was not a viable option. So there's no one. Well, on one side of the family there's no one, and on the other side of the family there's no one who cares. A Catch-22 that I'm all too familiar with. I'm hoping Silas can help me find a suitable foster family for him, so he can finish out the school year without too much upset. Once he turns eighteen, he can take possession of the property and we'll make sure there's a caretaker to look after things while he's at college."

She smiles tenderly and nods.

"He's going to veterinary school, and he starts an apprenticeship with Doc Ledo this Wednesday," I quickly add.

Amaryllis exhales and rubs my arm. "What a bright young man. So lucky to have you watching out for him, Mitzy. Now, I better get home and figure out what to make for dinner. Thanks for all the great wedding ideas. I'll be in touch."

As the alleyway door creaks closed, I rub my

mood ring absently. Maybe you could send me a nice little psychic message about the perfect foster family for Stellen? He can't live on my couch until graduation.

Cold black mists swirl within the glass dome of my antique mood ring.

No messages.

Not a single hint of help.

CHAPTER 8

WHEN SHERIFF HARPER shows up with our takeout feast, I'm busy working my way through a bag of chocolate-chip cookies and Stellen is parked in the Rare Books Loft poring over some anatomy reference books.

As I open the door, I give a little bow. "Good evening, Sheriff."

He glances at the nearly empty bag in my hands. "I hope you didn't ruin your appetite."

"You've met me, right?"

He chuckles and nods his agreement. "You want to grab some plates and forks? Are we eating up in the apartment?"

"We are. And, if you behave yourself, I'll even bring napkins."

His shoulders shake as he walks toward the wrought-iron spiral staircase.

Bringing up the rear, and having more than a passing obsession with film, I must get more information about this evening's entertainment. "So what epic big-screen sagas have you brought for us?"

Stellen looks up from his pile of reference material. "What time is it? Is it suppertime already?"

"You really are a bookworm. Don't tell Twiggy, but I'm giving you permission to leave all of your books on the reading table so you can continue your research tomorrow."

"Tomorrow I have to head back to school."

Erick shakes his head. "We all lost track of time, with the upsetting events of the weekend. It's winter break. There is no school."

"Right. I totally knew that. I've been— Everything's so— No school. Got it." Stellen leans back in the chair and runs one hand lovingly over the large volume open in front of him. "Perfect. I'll head straight over to the veterinary clinic in the morning, and I can keep reading when I get home."

Harper and I exchange a look of wonderment.

"Are you for real?" I shake my head in disbelief. "You've got to be the most studious teenager I've ever met."

Stellen shrugs and looks down.

Erick jostles the bags he's carrying. "Enough studying. Let's dig into this food and let the James Bond marathon begin."

I choke on my words and pat my chest to regain control. "James Bond? Seriously?"

Stellen pulls the candle handle and leads the way to the apartment. He grins as the bookcase door slides open. "I've seen all the Bond movies. Even though I was only three when *Casino Royale* came out, I streamed it and the other two before I saw *Spectre*, so I'd have the back story."

Placing a hand over my mouth, I shake my head in disbelief, but it's Erick who responds to the innocent oversight.

"I hate to be the one to break it to you, Stellen, but Daniel Craig is about the sixth actor to play James Bond. We're gonna kick it old-school tonight, and you're going to learn about the genealogy of Bond, while you're entertained."

Stellen flops onto the settee and looks at Erick as though he's crazy. "For real? There's other James Bonds?"

Erick inhales sharply and sets the food on the coffee table. He walks toward the VCR with his sack of tapes, pulls one out and holds it up for both of us to see. "Behold, Sean Connery, the original James Bond. Prepare for *Goldfinger*."

Passing out the plates and opening the takeout

containers, I'm pleased to see my favorite sweet-and-sour chicken among the main-course options, along with potstickers, egg rolls, and wontons. The man definitely knows a thing or two about my appetites.

Stellen picks up a plate, bites his lower lip, and whispers to me, "Which one do you want? I'll just have whichever one is left."

"You can have some of everything. That's the whole deal with Chinese food. Everything is up for grabs."

He stares at the variety of entrées, appetizers, and rice options and shakes his head. "You guys blow my mind on the daily." A half smile brightens his face as he glances toward Erick. "Thanks for all the food, Sheriff Harper. If you need me to do anything at the station, or wash your squad car, just let me know."

Erick pushes play, walks toward Stellen, and places a friendly hand on his shoulder. "You don't owe me anything. Any friend of Mitzy's is a friend of mine. You've got your hands full. Let us worry about your care and feeding for a while, okay?"

Stellen nods and loads a plate with our myriad options.

The piracy warning and the previews slide past, and I can't help but snicker as the familiar tune of the *Goldfinger* theme song fills the apartment.

Stellen is shocked and excited to learn the vast history behind the James Bond he grew up believing was the one and only.

The spy movies do their job and transport the young boy out of his world of misery and into the wonderful distraction of villains and gadgets.

I snuggle closer to Erick on the settee and he whispers softly in my ear, "What's that note on your corkboard about a helmet?"

And the dream of secret snuggles vanishes like a cartoon balloon that meets with an oversized straight pin. However, I don't miss the opportunity to lean closer and turn my lips toward his stubbled chin. "That was the one thing I forgot to tell you before. The racers who stopped by today mentioned that Jawbone was wearing a helmet, but there was no sled abandoned on the track."

Erick nods and turns toward me. "I'll look into it. Unfortunately, all the previous night's tracks were scraped away by the groomer, and no one runs a sled without gloves. I doubt we'll get any evidence, even if we figure out which snowmobile he might've used."

I nod and pull his arm tighter around my shoulders.

"Although, that does beg the question: How did you know the identity of the victim if he was wearing a helmet?"

My throat tightens and I search for a way to climb out of the corner I've painted myself into. "I don't remember. Someone must've recognized Jawbone's helmet or something."

A soft chuckle escapes from my boyfriend and he leans over and kisses my cheek. "Sure. That sounds very plausible, Moon."

Ignoring the implication, I point to the credits rolling up the television screen. "Time to put in the next one, Harper. We don't want the James Bond train to stop now!"

He teasingly tosses the blanket up over my head as he slides off the sofa to swap out the VHS tape.

By the time we get to Pierce Brosnan's Bond interpretation in *GoldenEye*, everyone is full, comfortable, and a little punchy. We crank the volume and our three voices badly belt out the theme song. Some of us know more of the words than others!

Right about the time we're going to hit the chorus for a second time, Grams rockets through the wall ready to launch a noise complaint, when—

Stellen's finger shoots in the air, and he points at the apparition and shouts, "Right there! Do you see it?"

I desperately try not to look at Grams, but the shock on her face is hard to ignore.

"He can see me? Mitzy, why didn't you tell me he could see ghosts?"

I fire off a quick thought message. *When was I going to tell you? I've been kinda busy with wedding planning, and it was only a suspicion that surfaced when we were searching for Pyewacket. He might've seen you at your writing desk in the printing museum. I couldn't exactly have a conversation with you then. What am I gonna do now?*

She crosses her bejeweled limbs and shakes her head. "I'd go with plausible deniability, dear."

Stellen sets his plate on the coffee table, chugs some soda to rinse down his broccoli beef, and gets to his feet. "She's right there. It looks like she's talking to you. Can't you see her?"

Erick shifts in the settee and fixes his eyes on me with anticipation.

"Her who? What do you think you see, Stellen?"

Grams nods. "Good. Good. Keep him on the ropes."

My ward looks from me to Ghost-ma and back again. "Seriously, she's talking to you right now. You can't hear it?"

The only thing that pleases me about this current disaster is that *he* can't hear it. "I'm not sure what you think you see, but shouldn't we get back to the movie?"

Erick leans forward as though he's got a suspect cornered. "I think the flick can wait. I'm pretty interested to hear more about what the kid thinks he sees."

I clench my jaw and fire off a warning to Grams. *Get out of here! If Stellen starts describing you—*

And my worst nightmare comes true.

"She's older."

Grams scoffs. "Older? The nerve of that kid."

Stellen continues. "She's got a real fancy dress on and lots of pearls, and some diamond rings."

Erick leans forward. "Sounds kind of familiar. Is the dress sort of a dark reddish-purple? Very expensive looking?"

Stellen nods. "Yeah, totally."

Ghost-ma fixes Stellen with an ethereal glare. "Can you believe this boy? He doesn't know a Marchesa when he sees one!"

I roll my eyes and force myself to look at anything except my grandmother's ghost.

Sheriff Harper narrows his gaze. "You said older, right?"

Stellen nods.

"Would you say she's in her sixties?"

The kid shrugs. "I'm not that good with age, or whatever. But I think ghosts can look different after they die. Maybe she was older and now her ghost is changing its appearance."

Grams arches a perfectly drawn brow. "This kid seems to know more about my realm than I do. Let's get him on the payroll, Mitzy."

"Give it a rest, Grams."

Erick drops his plate in his lap. "I knew it."

I clap my hand over my mouth, but it's too late. Every human— and ghost—in the room heard me. I lost my focus, and I said it out loud.

Stellen smiles brightly and puts a hand on my shoulder. "Did you hear? Because it looked like she was talking to you. Could you actually hear what she said?"

Isadora sighs dramatically. "You can't put this genie back in the bottle, sweetie."

The only thing that matters to me right now is the next words out of Erick's mouth. Is he going to think I'm a freak and walk out on me? Or will he be able to accept the part of me that's secretly been talking to my dead grandmother for more than a year?

Our eyes meet over the *moo goo gai pan*, and he shakes his head. "You could've told me, Moon. You could've trusted me." He sets his plate on the table, collects his coat, and strides out of the apartment.

Now I'm crying and Stellen is patting my back. "It's okay, Mitzy. I think there are more of us out there than you realize. Or maybe not. But I can see her, so you're not alone, you know?"

"Thanks, but I think I just blew up the only genuine relationship I've ever had."

"I've never been in a . . . or had a . . . I'm no relationship expert."

He pats my back again, and I wipe the stupid tears from my face.

Stellen looks over his shoulder. "Should I go talk to him or something?"

"Nah. He needs some time. He's right. I should've told him." A frustrated moan escapes me. The best thing I can do is keep busy. I'll distract myself with some otherworldly introductions. "Myrtle Isadora, this is Stellen Jablonski."

Grams gives the boy a friendly wave.

His eyes light up. "She waved to me."

She zooms through him, and I watch the goosebumps rise on his flesh.

"Whoa!" Stellen laughs out loud. "Yeah! She flew straight through me."

"Grams, he's not a toy. He's our guest. Give him privacy when he needs it and no thought-dropping."

She makes an "X" across her chest. "Cross my heart and hope to . . . Well, you get the idea."

I roll my eyes.

"I saw you moving that quill, up in the museum.

Can you do other stuff?" Stellen shoves another potsticker in his mouth while he awaits her demonstration.

She claps her ethereal hands with glee.

"I'll leave you two to get acquainted. I need to call Silas."

CHAPTER 9

DESPITE THE COMPLETE lack of blips on my psychic radar, I search the entire first floor of the bookshop for Erick before I call my mentor. Sure, it's a long shot, but I thought maybe he would be somewhere down here waiting for me to chase after him. Clearly, that's not his style.

Slouched on the rolly office chair in the back room, with my feet kicked up on the built-in desk, I call Silas and flick on the speaker.

"Good evening, Miss Moon. How may I assist?"

"I'd appreciate it if at no point during this conversation you say the words 'I told you so'."

"Understood. Proceed."

"Erick came by with dinner and movies. He was being really awesome to Stellen."

"I am pleased to hear that news. However, your tone indicates there is more to this story."

"How about I drop this tidbit, 'Stellen Jablonski can see ghosts,' and let you fill in the blanks."

Silas harrumphs, and in my mind's eye, I know he's carefully smoothing his bushy grey mustache.

"Did you hear what I said? Stellen can see Grams. He totally called me out in front of Erick."

"And what is the rest of the story, Mizithra?"

"Erick was kinda mad, and he stormed out." Slight exaggeration, but I'm looking for sympathy anywhere I can find it.

"Hmmm, for a psychic, with a fair degree more perceptive ability than the average human, your emotional vocabulary is stunted. Did Mr. Harper say anything before he left?"

"Yeah."

"Would you care to enlighten me?"

"Fine. He said I could've told him, that I could have trusted him."

"Ah, and there it is."

"Don't say it. Don't even think it."

"I have always counseled you to rely on truth as your best ally. I understand your misgivings, and your hesitancy to reveal your deepest secrets with abandon. However, I believe that what you are now experiencing is something we call the consequences of actions."

"Touché. Leave it to you to find the most elegant way possible to say I told you so. Yes, your alchemical wizardry reigns supreme. I should've been honest. I should've told Erick about the ghost thing. But I didn't. What am I supposed to do now?"

"A useful exercise, that I often employ, is to imagine one's self in the other party's circumstances."

"So I need to be an adult? You want me to imagine what it would be like if our situation was reversed?"

"Indeed. If Erick had been the one to keep such a vital secret at this stage of your relationship, how do you imagine that would affect your opinion of him?"

Silence hangs in the air between us as I struggle with *adulting*. Silas is right. He's always right. This is no exception. "I get it. I should've been honest with Erick when things started to get more serious. He suspected something was up, and I kept dodging. But it's too late now. The cat's out of the bag, and—"

"Ree-ow." Soft but condescending.

"Perhaps Robin Pyewacket Goodfellow is correct. You must bear this result until the tide shifts. Give Mr. Harper time and space. He's proven himself a good man, Mitzy. He will let you know when he's ready to discuss things."

"That's just it. I can't give him space. I promised Stellen I'd figure out who killed his dad. I'm bound to run into Erick on this case. What am I supposed to do then?"

"Maintain professional decorum. And let me know if there's anything I can do to assist."

Exhaling loudly, I almost end the call. "Oh, there is one thing. Stellen said that his father had several orders in process. Can you help him go through the receipts, or records, and contact the clients to have them pick up their carcasses, or whatever you call half-stuffed stuff?"

"I knew Mr. Jablonski to be quite meticulous in his record keeping. I shouldn't need the boy's help to fulfill this request."

"Well, there's a whole alarm system . . ." I laugh dryly. "Never mind. Alchemical transmutations should see you through. I'm sure an alarm system is nothing you can't handle. Thank you. I appreciate the advice, and Stellen will be relieved to hear that he doesn't have to go back to the taxidermy shop."

"Any time. Be sure to tell Isadora that I wish her well with her new friend."

Silas ends the call, and I lean back in the chair to think about his last words. She does have a new friend. I'm not the only person in the world who can see her now. I wonder if that means she'll love me less?

"Not on your life, young lady!"

The shock of her sudden appearance throws me off balance, and I flip over backward in the office chair.

She chuckles mercilessly, and two seconds later Stellen rounds the corner and his laughter joins hers.

"Great, now I have two humans and a ghost to laugh at my mishaps. Twiggy will be over the moon."

Grams ghost snorts, "No pun intended, I'm sure!"

Oh brother. I push myself to a seated position and rub my bruised elbow.

Stellen steps into the back room and clears his throat.

"Out with it, Jablonski."

He smiles and looks down at his feet. "I'm sorry I outed you in front of Erick. Isadora wrote it all down, and I guess you were trying to keep it secret. I can go down to the station and try to fix it for you."

"Hey, it's not your fault. You've been through enough. I'm a big girl. I can take care of myself. Let's enjoy the rest of our takeout and finish the movie marathon. You let me worry about Erick. Got it?"

He nods and points to the chair. "So, stuff like that happens to you all the time?"

"Yeah, I'm a klutz and a ghost hunter. It's a two-for-one deal."

He grins. "Sweet."

The soft buzzing of my cell phone on the bedside table wakes me. With one hand I reach for the phone and with the other for Pyewacket. One hand comes up empty.

The incoming call is from Silas, so I'll have to answer it. And I use the dim blue glow from the mobile to quickly search the room as I tiptoe to the bathroom.

Pyewacket is curled up on top of the soundly sleeping Stellen.

"Traitor," I whisper before closing the bathroom door.

"It's too early for etiquette, Silas. This better be important."

He harrumphs and draws a long breath. "What was the state of Mr. Jablonski's taxidermy building when you and the young boy departed?"

"The state of the building? What do you mean? It's a taxidermy shed. It was full of mounts, hides, some metal frames, tools . . . I don't know."

"And you're sure the boy secured the door and set an alarm?"

My extrasensory perception finally decides to

join the party, and a single word echoes in my mind. "Was there a break-in?"

"Ah, there is my ever-brilliant student. Indeed, there was. I had hoped to spare the boy another trip to this unsettling place, but in light of recent events, I will need his input. We must ascertain what was taken, and perhaps get the authorities involved."

The idea of facing Erick, especially on an empty stomach, doesn't sit well with me. "We'll grab a walking breakfast at the patisserie and join you in about thirty minutes. Is that all right?"

"It will have to be."

Setting down the phone, I splash warm water on my face and run my fingers through the haystack of hair looking back at me from the mirror.

As I approach the settee, Pye stares up at me with defiance.

"Look, Mr. Cuddlekins, I'm the one who knows where your favorite breakfast cereal is kept, so you best remember that when you're playing favorites."

I gently shake Stellen's shoulder. "Hey, buddy, we gotta get up."

He groans and rolls over.

Pyewacket leaps to safety and avoids getting pinned between the flip-flopping boy and the sofa cushions.

"See! I would never do that to you, ya Benedict Furball."

Looks like I'll have to take extreme measures. Returning to my bedside, I hit the button that rolls up the automatic blackout shades. The apartment is flooded with the bleak grey light of winter's morning.

Stellen yawns, stretches, and calls out without opening his eyes. "What time is it?"

"Time to go get some breakfast. There was a break-in at the taxidermy shed and Silas needs you to tell him if anything was stolen."

He sits up abruptly. "A break-in? Seriously? Is the cash missing?"

I shrug and roll my eyes. "How would I know that?"

He rubs his face and groans. "Right. Sorry. Mornings are tough."

"We've got that in common. Do you drink coffee?"

He chuckles. "No, but I might start today."

Inside Bless Choux, the line of patrons is astonishingly long considering the early hour. When Stellen and I finally reach the counter, the effervescent face of the patisserie's owner, Anne, falls on the boy.

She pinches her lips together and tilts her head downward. "How are you doing?"

Stellen shrugs, looks at the floor, and imperceptibly slides behind me.

Anne looks up at me. "I'm so sorry to hear about the tragedy, but it certainly is wonderful that you've taken him in."

Yeesh! There is no confidential living in this town. And now that Erick knows my secret, my life could get a whole lot more front-page.

"Mitzy? You drifted off, sweetie. What can I get you two?"

"I'll take a ginormous coffee and a slice of quiche." I tip my head over my shoulder. "What do you want?"

He mumbles something about whatever I'm having, so I place an amended order.

"And he'll have a half hot chocolate, half coffee and another slice of quiche." I pull a wad of cash out of my pocket, but Anne waves it away, almost angrily.

"Your money's no good here. You did a nice thing, and I'm returning the favor. Is this for here or to go, sweetie?"

"Unfortunately, it's to go today. Thanks."

Stellen and I step over to the display case containing travel mugs, holiday ornaments, and Bless Choux T-shirts.

He seems to be trying to shrink inside himself, and I recognize the fresh surge of pain that being out in public has caused.

"Don't worry. We'll be out of here in a second, and I promise no more shopping trips."

He leans toward me and stammers softly. "But I need . . . for the, you know."

"Right, a suit. After we take care of things with Silas, I can take you to Broken Rock for—"

He grips my arm urgently. "Can you just take me to the vet clinic? I don't care if the suit fits that good. Just guess my size. I'd really rather work with Doc Ledo today."

"No problem. I'll handle the shopping trip, and you can enjoy your first day of apprenticeship. Deal?"

He nods, and a flood of relief races across his face.

"To-go order for Mitzy Moon." The boisterous announcement bounces off the low ceiling.

Ignoring the tennis match-esque whipping of heads, I hand the bag containing our quiches to Stellen and grab our hot beverages. "Thanks, Anne."

The welcome blast of cold air on Third Avenue does wonders to relieve my embarrassment.

We load into the Jeep with our slices and wake-up juice and head out to the Jablonski's desolate place.

Silas was not idle while he waited for us to join

him. He's plowed through the order book and made half a page of notes.

"Thank you for agreeing to assist, young man. Is there anything missing?"

Before Stellen can answer, I blurt out my own observation. "The cat! That caracal that scared me half to death on Saturday . . . It's gone."

Stellen's well-trained eyes scour the contents of the shed. He nods in agreement. "You're right. There are also some expensive hides missing." He walks along the tool bench and I can almost feel him ticking off boxes on his mental inventory. "There are some tools missing. Nothing super valuable, but I thought I should mention it."

Silas nods. "Mention it all. You'd be surprised how the most insignificant things come to have great import."

He scans the space more slowly, shakes his head, and walks back toward Silas. "Three of the most valuable mounts are missing. *Eretmochelys imbricata, Panthera pardus orientalis,* and *Gymnogyps californianus.*"

My alchemical mentor nods as though speaking Latin is perfectly normal. He leans toward the ledger and runs his finger down the list. "I see no mention of a hawksbill turtle, an Amur leopard, or a California condor. Was your father working illegally? Those species are on the critically endangered list."

"No. No way. My dad always insisted on permits and letters from the U.S. Fish and Wildlife Service before he produced educational mounts."

Silas smooths his bushy grey mustache. "Why would they be missing?"

"Wait!" I step forward as the word "missing" rattles around inside my head. "Look. A page has been torn out of the ledger."

Stellen hurries to the desk and flips the pages back and forth. "Yep. There were at least six other orders on that missing page, including the caracal." He glances around a third time. "I don't think they took anything else, though."

"What about the money?" I ask.

Silas tilts his head and the furrows in his brow deepen.

"Stellen mentioned that his dad kept a lot of cash in the shed."

Stellen slides a stuffed mountain lion away from the back wall, kneels, and spins the combination on the safe back and forth. The door swings open and he breathes a sigh of relief. "Looks like it's all here. My dad and I were the only ones who knew where he kept the cash."

"Perhaps we should move the currency into a holding account while we settle the estate. The cash may not have been taken for a number of reasons. Not the least of which would be the difficulty in cracking that particular model of safe. However, if the intruder is determined, they may return."

Stellen nods and retrieves a small leather bag from beneath the workbench. He transfers the money into the bag and hands it to Silas.

I peer into the satchel and whistle. "Why did your father keep so much cash in here?"

He leans against the counter and sighs. "I told him it was dangerous. I told him we needed to get some kind of electronic payment system, but the wi-fi is super sketchy this far out of town, and he didn't want his clients to get mad. All of his transactions were in cash, or sometimes checks."

"I believe we must involve the authorities." Silas lifts his milky-blue eyes and raises one bushy eyebrow. "Shall I call the sheriff or will you, Mizithra?"

Crossing my arms over my chest, I shake my head and sigh. "You call him. I'll stay here and search for clues, while you take Stellen to the animal hospital." I turn to the boy. "Are you all right with Silas making the introductions?"

"Sure."

Silas gathers up the ledger and several other papers, shoves the lot into his dilapidated briefcase, and shuffles toward the door.

In his wake, I turn to Stellen and whisper, "Oh,

I should mention you'll have to ride in his 1908 Model T. You might want to grab a blanket or one of these pelts to keep warm." I chuckle at my joke, but the kid has a completely different reaction.

"Awesome. Can I crank it?"

"Follow me, young man. I'm pleased to see that someone from your generation appreciates history."

CHAPTER 10

As the guys sputter away from the Jablonski property in a slice of automotive history, the weight of my waiting settles over me like a dark cloud. This will be my first time seeing Erick since the *incident*, and it fills the pit of my stomach with dread.

Wandering back inside, I attempt to distract myself with some good old-fashioned investigative work. Since stress and worry are blocking my psychic abilities, and my cantankerous ring refuses to offer any assistance, I'm going to rely on my five regular senses.

Let's start with a visual inspection of the door.

Obvious signs of forced entry. Some type of crowbar or prybar was employed to wrench the door open, and a breaker was tampered with to disable the alarm. It stands to reason they could've picked the lock. It's a standard single-cylinder deadbolt. The thief chose the obvious break-in for one of two reasons: they were in a hurry; or they were attempting to disguise their true abilities.

Walking between the rows of creepy critters, I explore my theory further.

If their reasoning was distraction, maybe they took the additional items to hide the true target. Then, removing the page from the ledger, they assumed no one would be able to figure out which specific trophies went missing.

I run my hand along the workbench and pause. Why tools? Did they need the tools or was that another part of their plan to muddy the waters?

I'll check with Stellen and see if he knows exactly which tools were taken.

Also, if the stolen mounts were endangered animals, they would be worth a fortune on the black market. That points to financial motivation.

Tires crunching down the snowy drive break my concentration and send a fresh wave of nausea through my gut.

Should I wait here? Should I greet them out front? I'd prefer to disappear, but I don't currently possess enough calm or focus to do anything but mildly hyperventilate.

Hurrying to the front of the shop, I have the displeasure of being greeted by none other than the trigger-happy Deputy Paulsen.

"Birch County Sheriffs, we're coming in. Hands where I can see them."

"Paulsen, it's me. I'm the one who called this in."

"False. Silas Willoughby called in the break-in."

"Well, I was here when he called it in." I scoff and roll my eyes. "Don't shoot, I'm leaving." In my haste to slip past her short, squat frame, I nearly crash into Erick. I school my features into a calm I don't possess and keep my tone professional. "Sheriff Harper."

His response is equally cloaked in disinterest. "Miss Moon. We'll take it from here."

I open my mouth to protest, but I have no bargaining power.

Erick gestures toward my vehicle. "You're free to go. Please let Mr. Willoughby know that there is a copy of the ME's report waiting for him at the station."

"Don't you need a statement from me?"

"Not at this time. Once we conduct our investigation and ascertain the scope of the burglary, we may follow up. Until then, you're free to go."

"Copy that." Trudging through the snow toward my vehicle, I feel like Atlas, and the weight of the world is crushing me. The hurt in Erick's eyes will haunt me all day.

I'm fresh out of ideas on how to fix my messed up relationship, so I'll head back to the bookshop and see if Silas can get his hands on that report. Maybe the additional information about time of death and cause of death will unblock my extrasensory perceptions.

Slipping my cell phone in the bracket clipped to the heater vent, I call Silas and place it on speakerphone.

"Good morning, Mitzy. Did the sheriff arrive at the Jablonski's?"

"Yeah."

"It would appear the encounter was less than satisfactory."

"Understatement of the century."

"Were you able to uncover any useful information before the deputies arrived?"

"Hardly. The stress and worry sent my psychic senses packing. Forced entry, and some theories about the motivation, but nothing else."

Silas pauses to contemplate my meager offering. "Never underestimate the fragments that you gather. The devil is in the details."

Yawning with boredom, I struggle to move the focus away from the detritus that is my personal life. "There's a copy of the medical examiner's report waiting for you at the station. Do you want me to meet you there?"

"I'm currently conducting research at your bookshop. I shall retrieve the report during my luncheon interval."

"Copy that. See you in ten."

As I cross the Rare Books Loft, Silas looks up from his stacks of papers. "Ah, at last. May I use your apartment for a brief experiment?"

"Why not?" Opening the door, I step out of the way as Silas transfers the Jablonski ledger from an oak reading table to my coffee table.

He plants himself in the scalloped-back chair and nods for me to close the bookcase.

Taking my standard position on the settee, I lean forward, ready for the action. "Whatcha doin'?"

Silas ignores my playful query and pulls items from the secret pockets within his tattered tweed jacket.

Rubbing my hands together, I grin eagerly. "Oooh, is someone doin' some alchemy?"

"I'll thank you to take this seriously, Mizithra Achelois Moon."

Oops. Formal name territory. I crossed the line. "Understood. May I observe?"

"Certainly."

He opens the ledger and runs his finger along the torn edge of the missing page.

I gasp. "Are you going to summon the page from the ether?"

"Must I continually remind you of the differences between magic and alchemy?"

Sitting back, I cross my arms. "No. Carry on."

He selects a stem of dried herb and shows it to me. "Mugwort."

I nod.

Silas lights the dried twig of mugwort with the snap of his fingers, and I have to throw a hand over my mouth to keep from exclaiming my admiration. Luckily, my psychic senses detect his secret satisfaction. I'm starting to understand his subdued, showboating nature.

He lets the ash fall into a small silver bowl and picks up a second vial filled with a crimson powder.

"Crushed dragon's blood."

I open my mouth, but a single commanding finger stops me from speaking. "It is a root, not a mythical animal's dried blood."

Closing my maw, I swallow awkwardly. It's almost as though he can read my mind.

He circles the first two fingers of his left hand

above the bowl and the dark ashes and red powder swirl together. Carefully lifting the bowl with his right hand, he sprinkles it lightly over the right-hand page of the ledger.

My eyes widen in anticipation.

Once the powder is distributed, he waves his right hand over the book. The fine grains align like a formation of micro-soldiers marching over the page. He then lifts the book to his eye-level and gently exhales across the paper. The dust quivers and quakes over the page.

My jaw drops open as I watch the granules fall into the crevasses that appear on the sheet's surface.

When the motion ceases, he lowers the book to the table. "I fear success is not in our pantheon on this day."

Circling around to his side of the table, I kneel in front of the book. I can see where the substance has fallen into the marks caused by the pen pressing through the missing page and into this sheet that was left behind. However, whoever wrote those entries had a gentle hand. The marks are shallow and few.

I flop onto the floor, cross my legs, and gaze up at the alchemist. "Is that your best trick?"

He harrumphs and glares at me.

"I mean, do you have another idea? I know I said the wrong thing. Don't look at me like that."

His fiery gaze continues to bore a hole through my snark. "That was indeed my best trick, as you so eloquently put it."

Shrugging, I offer some encouragement. "We pretty much know what was taken. Maybe Stellen will remember the other two entries from that page, but for now the theme is clearly valuable endangered species. Let's just run with that."

He leans against the chair and laces his fingers over his round belly. "Indeed. At least we have that fragment."

"Oh shoot! I forgot. I have to get a suit for Stellen. He needs something to wear to the funeral."

Without missing a beat, my mentor has the answer. "You'll be wanting to see Rivail Gustafson in Broken Rock. He is the proprietor of A Stitch in Time."

"Of course you know a tailor. However, I don't care how many stitches he can make in time, he can't make a suit in time for this funeral."

"While he specializes in bespoke menswear, he will also have a selection of off-the-rack vestments for your perusal."

"Yeesh." While the word bespoke always makes me cringe internally, I don't share this with Silas.

Instead, I take his recommendation without retort. "I'm on it. By the way, how'd it go at the clinic?"

He makes a sound that could be construed as pleasant. "Quite well. Doctor Ledo is thrilled to have help, and Stellen's passion for the profession would be obvious to even a casual observer. You've done a good thing, Mitzy."

"Well, that still leaves me in the losing column, but it's something to build on."

"Once you allow yourself to trust in the sheriff's true nature, a solution will present itself."

I can barely prevent my eyes from rolling dramatically. "Thanks for the info about the tailor. Will you still be here when I get back?"

"Indeed. We shall discuss the report and perhaps your gifts will grace us with some guidance."

"Sounds good. See you later."

Once inside the Jeep, I type in the name of the tailor's shop and let my GPS take over. The drive along the Black Cap Trail, past Pancake Bay, provides a magnificent distraction. The intricate ice floes and the beautiful snow-dusted scenery succeed in taking my mind off my problems for a short while.

A Stitch in Time is an inviting slice of history. A cleverly painted exterior and the faux-thatched roof harken back to images of an old European village. The wares displayed in the window show careful craftsmanship and pride in product.

As I open the door, a lovely bell tinkles. Nothing brash, nothing off-putting—a light, welcoming sound that makes me feel cared for.

A willowy wisp of a man strides from the back room. His wild mop of white hair rivals my own, and his astonishing mustache must hold several world records.

"Good afternoon. Welcome to A Stitch in Time. What may I create for you today?"

This definitely seems like the type of establishment where name-dropping is essential. "Good afternoon. Silas Willoughby referred me."

"Ah, yes. That sly old fox. He's due for a new suit, most assuredly."

All I can think is that Silas was due for a new suit about twenty years ago, but Grams has taught me that "more flies with honey" is the best approach. "I'll definitely remind him. However, today I am here to buy something off the rack."

His shoulders and mustache sag simultaneously.

It's all I can do not to laugh out loud. "I'm caring for a young man who lost his father this past weekend, and he needs a suit for the funeral."

No sooner are the words out of my mouth than

the man's entire aura shifts. His eyes sharpen, his mustache perks up, and he adjusts the cloth tape measure draped around his shoulders as though it were an ermine stole.

"My condolences to your young friend. Right this way, Miss—"

"Moon. Mitzy Moon." My recent Bond marathon has had an unfortunate side effect.

"Ah, your reputation precedes you, Miss Moon. You are the granddaughter of the illustrious Isadora Duncan, are you not?"

"If you're referring to Myrtle Isadora Johnson Linder Duncan Willamet Rogers, then yes, I am she."

His knowing smile marks him as one of my grandmother's many "special friends." "A lifetime ago . . ." He smiles wistfully and sighs. "Shall we focus on the task at hand? What is the boy's size?"

I chew my bottom lip. "I'm not great with sizes. He's a junior in high school, if that helps?"

Mr. Gustafson chuckles and fluffs one end of his luxurious mustache. "Why don't you describe him to me, and I shall do my best. Let's start with height."

A series of images flash through my mind. "He's about here, just below my nose."

Mr. Gustafson whips the tape measure from his shoulders and flourishes it in front of me. "Five feet and six inches. And about how wide are the boy's shoulders?"

The focus on the task at hand allows a flicker of a psychic replay to pass through, and I can see Stellen standing in front of me in my mind's eye. "About the same as mine."

Another flourish of the tape measure. "And is he a thick boy or more of a waif?"

"He's quite thin. He eats like a horse, but he's skinny as a rail."

"I imagine he's not done growing. I should think he'll have quite a growth spurt in the next year or two." Gustafson struts over to the rack with the confidence and grace of a runway model and selects three items. "Do you prefer a traditional black, a charcoal, or a midnight blue?"

"I suppose we should stick with tradition."

"And the boy's coloring? Perhaps we can pull a bit of color into the shirt or tie, to offset the harsh effects of such a deep color."

"His hair is dark brown, curly, and his eyes are green with little flecks of gold."

Mr. Gustafson's mustache wiggles as he smiles broadly. "You are exceptionally observant. An excellent trait."

He runs his finger over the rows of neckties and selects a deep green, with tiny black and gold fleur-de-lis. "Now, to pair this with the proper shirt." A moment later, he has selected three options and shuffles through them. He tests the tie and the coat with each combination. "I believe the dark green gives us the most bang for our buck, while remaining subtle and respectful. Would you not agree?"

Don't get me started. "I think that's fantastic. I'll take all of it." As I walk toward the counter, a surge of generosity washes over me. "If I wanted to get a gift for Silas, what would you recommend?"

Mr. Gustafson winks at me and takes a little bow. "What a lovely thought. I would highly recommend a silk pocket square. Mr. Willoughby is a huge fan of the perfectly folded pocket square."

This news hardly surprises me, but I'm happy to have the opportunity to repay a portion of my mentor's kindness. "Would you select one for me and add it to the order?"

"Of course."

He carefully packages the items with tissue and gold seals, and fits the suit into a garment bag.

That's when it dawns on me that I definitely don't have enough cash for this transaction. I pull out the plastic and offer it hesitantly. "Do you accept this form of payment?"

He waves it away. "Isadora has an account with me. She's no longer with us, God rest her magnificent soul, but I'm sure none of the particulars have changed."

"Well, I'm sure you're correct." Having visited the bank in Pin Cherry Harbor back when I first arrived, I was shocked to learn about passbooks and NCR paper in the town that tech forgot. It makes perfect sense that none of the account numbers would've changed. "I hope I have another reason to visit you, Mr. Gustafson. You've been more than helpful."

"I wish the same, my dear." He hands me the garment bag, and another carefully wrapped parcel. "Again, my condolences."

"Thank you."

Silas is returning from his "luncheon interval" by the time I get back to the Bell, Book & Candle.

"What does the report say?"

"We shall examine it together." Silas takes a seat at one of the reading tables in the Rare Books Loft and lays the report on the polished oak surface.

"Time of death?"

"Estimated time of death is between 8:00 and 10:00 p.m. on Friday evening."

"And they're taking into account the weather, the body being buried in snow, all that stuff, right?"

"Indeed. They list the details of the factors used in the calculation in a footnote."

"And what about cause of death?"

Silas moves his gnarled finger down the page and shakes his head with displeasure. "Gruesome. Perhaps it is best if we simply refer to it as a stabbing and gloss over the details."

He turns the paper toward me and taps a finger on the description.

My expression grows more horrified with each sentence. "Ew. That's so . . . violent. Also, it was either a super lucky strike, or the attacker knew exactly where to stab someone for the quickest result."

Silas nods. "While the unfortunate snowmobile collision with the corpse has obscured some evidence, at this juncture I believe we must entertain both scenarios."

"Does the other report mention if they found a murder weapon on scene?"

He peruses the attached crime-scene report and shakes his head. "No murder weapon has been located, and they refer to the place where the body was discovered as a possible dump site. The suspicion seems to lean toward a working theory that the murder took place elsewhere, and Mr. Jablonski was placed in the deep snow beside the track, likely in the hopes that the body wouldn't be uncovered until spring. Possibly the assailant assumed decomposition and predation would prevent discovery altogether."

"What are the specs on the alleged murder weapon?"

"They're hypothesizing a screwdriver, with at least a nine-inch shank." Silas holds his hands apart to show me a visual estimation of the length.

"That definitely points to someone involved in the snowmobile racing world, wouldn't you say?"

"A likely assumption. However, without an actual murder weapon, it would be difficult for the authorities to make an arrest. Perhaps you can inspect the report and see if you receive any additional messages."

I scan through the medical examiner's report and the crime-scene report, but my psychic senses continue their vacation. "Nothing. Nada. Bupkus." If I have any intention of receiving extrasensory help on this investigation, it seems like I'm going to have to patch things up with Erick. The stress and the constant roiling in my gut are blocking any and all access to any of the four "clairs."

"When Stellen returns from the animal hospital, perhaps he can recall some additional details about his father's coaching. I would be interested to know if Trey Lee's father made any visits to the Jablonski property."

"Right? It sure seems like he would've been

upset about losing such an excellent coach, when his son was poised to take the title and collect all that prize money."

Silas smooths his mustache with a thumb and forefinger. "You are correct." He hums for a moment before leaning forward in anticipation. "Were you successful in your visit to A Stitch in Time?"

"Geez! I left everything in the car! I'll be right back."

Thundering down the wrought-iron staircase, I'm met by the scowling face of Twiggy at the bottom of the stairs.

"Look, doll, you're disturbing the customers. Maybe you can stop running around like a herd of elephants and let people shop in peace."

I glance around the deserted first floor and stifle a chuckle. "I'll do my best." Before we get into an argument about disturbing invisible customers, I hurry out the side door and retrieve the packages from the Jeep.

"Mr. Gustafson is so skilled with his tape measure. I hope the suit fits Stellen."

Silas nods. "I'm certain you meant to say that you hope it *still* fits him in the spring?"

"What do you mean *still*?"

"Ah yes. I continue to underestimate your lack of experience in the customs of the far north. In a land where permafrost often reaches four feet deep and grave markers are obscured by layers of snow, the burials for deaths occurring in January, February, and March are almost always postponed until late April or early May. Memorial services and cremations are conducted during the winter, but we postpone interments. I will review Mr. Jablonski's last wishes, but I believe he was slated for burial, which will take place in the spring."

My jaw hangs open like that of a broken ventriloquist dummy. "What do you mean postponed? Like, there's just a room full of bodies somewhere, waiting for spring? You can't be serious?"

Silas tilts his head and fixes me with an iron gaze. "Mizithra, when have you known me to jest? The realities of our brutal winters cannot be ignored. Mortuaries have storage vaults, and storing the deceased during the harshest months of winter is a common practice. Do not fret. I'm sure Mr. Gustafson can adjust the hem on the trousers if young Stellen happens to hit a growth spurt before the service."

My gums flap a bit, like those of a fish out of water, and I almost forget the gift. Almost. Reaching into the bag, I retrieve a small tissue-wrapped parcel held together by a lovely golden seal. "Here. I got you this."

Silas straightens his spine and a look of surprise grips him. "What is this? A gift? The Yuletide has passed. Why would you present me with this token?"

A self-satisfied smile finally overrides my flapping jaw, and I nod happily. "Don't act so surprised. Do I need a reason to get you a present?"

"Perhaps not. I'm not one to make a fuss."

"Well, I'm making a fuss. Thank you for all your excellent mentoring!"

Silas harrumphs into his mustache, suppresses his emotions, and continues to unwrap his present. "What a lovely pocket square. Exactly what I needed to perk up this old coat."

He removes a tattered grey pocket square from his ancient tweed jacket and replaces it with the lovely navy-blue silk square that Mr. Gustafson carefully folded for me.

"That looks great, Silas. Do you like it?"

He fumbles unnecessarily with the item and clears his throat twice. "It is a thoughtful and welcome gift. Thank you, Mizithra."

"You're welcome. I'll spare you the embarrassment of a big hug, but you should know that I think you deserve one."

He tugs at his jacket, smooths his mustache, and shuffles the papers on the table.

Poor little guy. I've embarrassed him with my sappy comments. I'm all too familiar with the discomfort of raw emotion. I'll spare him any further agitation. "I guess I'll head over to the station and see if they're bringing Mr. Lee in for questioning."

"A wonderful idea. I shall continue my efforts with the Jablonski estate paperwork." He pats the stack of legal documents and leans forward studiously.

CHAPTER 11

BUNDLING UP FOR THE SHORT TREK, I play through various movie scenarios inside my head. When I open the door of the station, will Erick sense my arrival and step out of his office? Will he be happy to see me, or will he banish me from the premises?

Maybe I should've taken the time to put on a sexy outfit or a seductive shade of lipstick?

All the handy little gimmicks that work so well on the silver screen seem like empty, hollow gestures. The truth is, my heart is broken and I owe Sheriff Harper a massive apology. No plunging neckline or luscious berry lip tint is going to solve this problem.

Inside the bustling station, two deputies are fielding calls and making notes in the bullpen, while Furious Monkeys has had to put her phone down to handle the growing line of real, live humans queuing up in front of her desk, to file complaints about the canceled snocross or offering useless tips in an attempt to score a juicy tidbit to share with their coffee klatch. She fires me a put-upon side eye and nods her head sharply. Clearly, she hasn't heard that Erick and I are on a break.

Taking any opportunity given, I push through the crooked swinging gate and enter the bullpen.

Just when I think I'll make it safely across the room, Deputy Paulsen launches out of Erick's office with a red face and veritable steam coming out of her ears. "What are you doing here, Moon?"

When in doubt, lie it out. "I had some information for Deputy Johnson." Deputy Johnson and I are loosely acquainted, and he mostly knows me as the sheriff's girlfriend, so he fidgets nervously behind his desk as his eyes dart back and forth between Deputy Paulsen and myself. A tentative smile finally breaks his stern expression. "Give me one second to finish this gentleman's statement, Miss Moon."

Nodding pleasantly, I flash a grin and offer a triumphant head nod in Paulsen's direction. "Looks like everything will be handled in a moment. Don't let me keep you from your investigation."

She growls openly and storms through the front of the station.

Johnson pulls the report out of his typewriter, grabs a pen, and hands it to the concerned citizen. "Just sign your name at the bottom, and you're free to go. Thank you for coming in today." He looks up and gestures his thumb toward the interrogation rooms. "Sheriff Harper is questioning a suspect right now. Did you want to wait in his office?"

Not bad for a newbie. For a minute there, I thought Johnson actually believed my story. But clearly he saw through my ruse and kindly chose to support my alibi. "Actually, that sounds great. Thanks for covering for me."

He rolls his eyes ever so slightly and winks.

Walking toward Erick's office, I'm overcome with curiosity about whom he's questioning. A quick glance over my shoulder reveals Deputy Johnson deep in conversation with the concerned citizen. Before he can look up, I slip into the observation room between Interrogation Rooms One and Two. Activating extreme stealth mode, I flip the silver switch above the speaker and hold my breath . . .

"Look, Mr. Lee. We know that Coach Jablonski was leaving your team to coach Priest. With your son poised to win $75,000 on the circuit, I don't think you could afford to lose a coach, and you certainly couldn't afford a coach as good as Jablonski to defect to a competitor's team."

Mr. Lee rubs his hands together and leans forward, his face a mask of worry. "Sheriff, please, you have to believe me. I went to the track Friday night on good terms with Jablonski. Jawbone had given Trey every advantage, but Trey had outgrown him. The fact that he was moving on to coach Priest was a mutual decision. We had a conversation, I told him I understood, and he offered us a refund."

"And now that he's dead, my deputy noted that you've hired an attorney to recover those coaching fees."

Mr. Lee exhales in frustration and leans back. "Sure. But only after I found out about his death. We had a gentlemen's agreement. There was no reason for me to kill him."

"The evidence points to the attacker having more than a cursory knowledge of anatomy. The blow that killed Mr. Jablonski was expertly placed at the base of the skull. Death would've been nearly instantaneous, with very little blood loss. I'm sure you can understand how incriminating that is, Mr. Lee. You're a doctor. A surgeon, if I'm not mistaken. Precisely placing that incision would've been second nature for you. I have deputies up on the mountain searching for the murder weapon. I'm afraid if we find your prints on it, we will make an arrest."

Mr. Lee bends forward, places his elbows on the metal table, and hangs his head in his hands.

I lean toward the glass in an attempt to hear his soft whisper.

"Sheriff, my boy is in the hospital with severe injuries. He could be paralyzed. He could have suffered brain damage." The man lifts his head and gazes directly at the sheriff. "I have a temper, I'll admit to that. Maybe I wasn't happy when Jablonski told me he was going to quit coaching Trey. But I promise you, we parted on good terms Friday night. He was alive and well when I left him on that mountain. Now please, can I go back to the hospital and sit with my son?"

My forehead bumps the glass, and I jump back and inhale sharply. The intense emotion of Mr. Lee's last statement caused me to lose my spatial awareness.

Erick's shoulders tense and it doesn't take a psychic to guess that he suspects *someone* of eavesdropping. He hastily gets to his feet. "You're free to go, Mr. Lee. We'll be in touch as the investigation develops."

Mr. Lee slowly stands. His shoulders are slumped and his spirit is broken. "I understand,

Sheriff." He walks out of the interrogation room and Erick spins towards the one-way glass.

Busted.

There's no point in running, he'll step out of that door and intercept me before I make it two steps down the hallway. Better to sit tight and take my lumps like a big girl.

He strides out of the interrogation room and my stomach swirls uncomfortably.

I fix my eyes on the door handle of the observation room, but it doesn't twist. I lean toward the one-way glass and try to see around corners, but there's no sign of Sheriff Harper.

Well, I'm not going to sit in here like a child in timeout.

Taking a deep breath, I square my shoulders and open the door. The short hallway outside the interrogation rooms is empty, and the door to Sheriff Harper's office is tightly closed.

Message received.

I stalk out of the station and stomp down Main Street toward my bookshop.

The nerve of that guy! It's not like I cheated on him or lied about being married before! I kept a little secret about a ghost living in my bookstore. Is it really that bad?

The cell phone in the pocket of my puffy coat

rings and the shock wave sends a flash of guilt across my face.

"Stellen? Is everything all right?"

"Everything was amazing. Doc Ledo is the best. Should I walk back to your apartment, or is someone picking me up?"

I thunk my head with the heel of my mitten. "I'll be there in five minutes." Stuffing the phone back in my pocket, I pick up the pace and hop into the Jeep. Having a kid is more work than I imagined. I completely forgot that Stellen was at his apprenticeship. What if he was only two or three years old? He wouldn't know what to do. He wouldn't know whom to call. It's official, I'd be a terrible mother. Maybe I'm just one of those people who's not cut out for long-term relationships or procreation. Maybe I'm destined to be a lonely, selfish, secret-keeping spinster.

Taking the final turn at an unsafe speed, the Jeep fishtails as I round the corner onto Gunnison Avenue. Shockingly, my instinct to counter steer is the correct one, and I get the vehicle under control.

When I turn into the parking lot of the Animal Hospital, Stellen is waiting outside.

"Thanks for coming to get me, Mitzy, but I can totally walk next time. You don't have to change your plans for me."

"Nonsense! And next time, wait inside. It's freezing out here."

"Inside? My dad always liked me to wait outside, so I wouldn't waste his time when he picked me up from stuff. With the coaching and the taxidermy gigs, he really didn't like making trips into town for no reason."

To hear the young boy refer to himself as "no reason" breaks my heart. I have no right to judge Mr. Jablonski, but I'm going to. This sweet, sensitive kid lost his mother to a horrible disease, and his father offered him nothing in the way of comfort. A roof over his head is not what this little soul needed. "I don't mean this to sound harsh, Stellen. I'm sure your father was dealing with his own pain surrounding your mother's illness. But you're important, and you deserve a good life. Don't ever think of yourself as an inconvenience. All right?"

He gazes out the passenger-side window and nods his head.

"I'll see how long this temporary custody thing will last, but no matter what type of foster home you have to go to, never give up on yourself. You're gonna graduate, and you're absolutely going to veterinary school. Promise me you won't let the system break you."

Stellen's small Adam's apple struggles to

swallow the emotion welling up inside him. "I don't think my dad was upset when my mom died."

The words slice into my heart like a hot knife through butter. "Why would you say that? I'm sure he loved your mom."

Stellen sniffles and continues, "Maybe. After she passed away, all he ever talked about was the mountain of medical bills. The reason he had to work so hard, and take on so many taxidermy projects, was because of her. He always used to say that the cancer was the worst thing that ever happened to him."

My hand smacks against the steering wheel, and I exhale. "Well, he was wrong. What your mother went through was terrible. She fought it as long as she could so that she could be there for you. Every treatment she endured was to buy a few more days with you. And if your father didn't appreciate that, and he thinks it was money wasted, then maybe he got what was coming to him."

Stellen's eyes widen in shock and he hugs his arms around his torso.

Pulling into the garage, I turn the engine off and wipe the stream of tears from my cheeks. "I'm sorry. I don't know where that came from. It's none of my business, and I'm sure your dad did the best he could."

Stellen tentatively reaches out a hand and

places it on my arm. "I think you're right. I know you're not supposed to speak ill of the dead, or whatever, but—"

Our tear-filled eyes meet, and I finish his sentence. "You'd pay any amount of money to have just one more day with her."

Stellen nods, and I offer him a hug.

After drying our eyes, we head into the bookshop to discover Amaryllis and Twiggy deep in an argument, and the volume is growing.

"Like I told you before, we ain't moving nothin'."

"Don't be ridiculous, Twiggy. How are we going to fit guests in here with all of these bookshelves in the way?"

"Run the chairs between the aisles." Twiggy places a defiant fist on her hip.

Amaryllis gestures wildly. "And how will they see?"

I lean toward Stellen and whisper, "You see what you can find to eat in the back room, and I'll throw some water on this fire."

He smirks and nods.

"Ladies, may I offer my assistance?"

Twiggy turns on me. "Look, kid, I told you I'd handle this. We have a creative difference. I'll take care of it."

Amaryllis shoots me a pleading stare, and right

as I'm about to put my foot down with Twiggy, an enraged ghost rockets down from the mezzanine.

Grams heads straight for Twiggy, and instead of passing through her, she freeze-frames. The prolonged ghost chills send Twiggy into a violent shiver. "Is it Isadora? Tell her to get off me!"

I wait a beat, like any good movie villain. "Isadora? Don't force me to deface one of your designer gowns."

Grams finally finishes passing through Twiggy and floats behind her. The shimmering features hold an expression full of menace, and Ghost-ma is ready to dish out additional retribution at a moment's notice.

"Twiggy, I don't know how to tell you this, but I get the distinct feeling that if you don't do exactly what Amaryllis says, Grams is seriously planning on possessing you."

Twiggy makes the sign of the cross with her fingers and backs away from me. "You tell that ungrateful Myrtle Isadora that she'll lose her last friend if she doesn't keep her creepy ghost fingers off me."

Grams crosses her arms over her ample bosom and winks.

"You're really not in any position to bargain. Why don't you hire a company that you trust to box up the books, and we'll store them in a weatherproof, safe location, and then we'll let Amaryllis make all the decisions about decorating the main floor for her wedding? Do we have a deal, Twiggy?"

Twiggy frantically searches the air around her and rubs the gooseflesh on her arms. "Nothin' gets packed up without my supervision."

"Absolutely. I wouldn't have it any other way. Hire whoever you want and send me the bill."

Twiggy makes no further argument. She shakes her head and stomps her biker boots with unnecessary force as she heads into the back room to make the arrangements.

Amaryllis sighs with relief and offers me a namaste-style bow of gratitude. "You got here just in time. That woman was driving me crazy. Can you imagine? Guests sitting in little rows as though they were riding a train, not able to see anything? It's enough to drive a woman to drink."

"I hear ya. However, Grams deserves all the thanks. I wouldn't know the first thing about running this bookstore without Twiggy, so I have to tread lightly, but I think Isadora's little stunt gave us the bargaining power we needed. If there are any other issues that come up, just let me know. Twiggy's a good person, she's just kinda set in her ways, you know?"

Amaryllis nods too easily. "Speaking of people who are set in their ways, Jacob is still living under the misguided impression that I kept the guest list small. Do you think I can wedge a hundred chairs in here?"

I chuckle and shake my head. "I guess you'll find out. I need to call Silas. Is there anything else I can help you with?"

She hooks her arm through my elbow and smiles from ear to ear. "Just one thing."

"Name it."

"Will you be my maid of honor?"

An entire movie montage of horrible bridesmaid's dresses flashes before my eyes. "Sure. Of course."

She breathes a sigh of relief and squeezes my arm. "I'm so glad you said that, because I already bought your dress. I hope it fits!"

Dear Lord baby Jesus. "I'm sure it will."

"Perfect, I'll bring it by, and you can try it on and we'll talk about what we're going to do with your hair."

"Sounds great." I clumsily disengage my arm and head upstairs before I say something I'll regret. Bridesmaid's dresses? Hairdos? Heaven help me! How do I get myself into these things?

CHAPTER 12

THE SECRET BOOKCASE SLIDES OPEN, and, as I walk into the apartment, I experience the distinct feeling of being watched. Spinning around, I find Pyewacket perched atop the antique armoire with one eye open. His golden orb is fixed on me with a mixture of impatience and doubt.

"Sorry to keep you waiting, Mr. Cuddlekins. I had to pick up our houseguest and prevent an attack of Bridezilla. But I'm here now. How can I be of service?"

The large tan ball of muscle leaps from the wardrobe and lands with the grace of a prima ballerina. He drops onto his haunches, stares intently, but makes no vocalization.

Walking toward the fiendish feline, I crouch

and await further instruction. "I'm here. I'm listening, but you're not telling me anything."

His black-tufted ears twitch, and he leans forward.

I instinctively offer my palm as he drops a small item from his mouth. "I'm going to go out on a limb and assume this has something to do with my case?"

"Reow." Can confirm.

I roll the red shard back and forth in my hand and shrug. "I've got nothing, Pyewacket. I mean, it looks plastic, but other than that—"

"How's the investigation going?"

I can't believe I didn't hear the door slide open. I must've been focusing harder than I thought. However, despite my best efforts, my psychic senses are still on the fritz. "Hey, Stellen, we got the reports from the sheriff's station." I place the chunk of red debris on the coffee table, stand, and brush some cat hair from my knee.

The boy flops onto the settee with a bowl of Fruity Puffs.

Shockingly, Pyewacket neither comments nor attacks.

Stellen swallows his mouthful of sugary cereal. "What'd the medical examiner say?"

"Are you sure you're okay to talk about this?"

He shrugs and sets his snack bowl on the table. "I don't know. Not talking about it isn't going to change anything. Maybe knowing the truth will help me deal, you know?"

"Yeah, I understand. If you change your mind, though, it's okay to tell me to stop talking."

Grams bursts through the wall, already chuckling. "Well, good luck with that task. Tell him what I said, Mitzy."

Rolling my eyes, I pick up my duties as an afterlife interpreter. "Grams thinks that it's too great a task to get me to stop talking."

Stellen gazes at the elegant ghost hovering above us and grins. "It's so cool that she's here all the time."

Sighing, I know he's thinking about his mother, and the only way I can change the topic is to talk about his dead dad. Wow, what a great option. "The medical examiner places time of death Friday night between 8:00 and 10:00 p.m."

Stellen laces his fingers behind his head and stretches out on the sofa. "Makes sense. That was part of my dad's ritual. Every night before a big race, he'd wait until the venue had cleared out and then he would ride the track, as well as walk the track. Both the drag track and the snocross track. He said it was to check for imperfections, but I think he was superstitious. One time when I was sick and my mom was in the hospital, he had to stay home with me and didn't get to perform the ritual inspection. Trey had his only loss of the season the next day."

"So you didn't think anything about him being out late?"

"Nope."

"What about in the morning? Didn't you wonder where he was at breakfast?" I tilt my head.

Stellen shakes his head sadly. "We didn't really eat together, you know?"

My heart squeezes with pain and I'm at a loss for words.

Pyewacket casually climbs onto the coffee table and brazenly plunges his face into the unprotected bowl of Fruity Puffs.

Stellen smiles. "They're all yours, boy. Sorry I didn't ask."

Pye lifts his head and squeezes his eyes closed as he stares at the usurper.

"Well, he didn't yell at you, and he didn't thwack you with his razor-sharp claws. I think he actually likes you."

Stellen reaches a hand toward the caracal's arched back.

"Wait! Do not touch him when he is eating. I mean, not to be that person, but—"

Stellen chuckles. "Thanks. I owe you one. The last thing I need is an injured hand when Doc Ledo is giving me so much responsibility at the clinic."

He chews the edge of his fingernail and stares at the tin-plated ceiling. "Did they have a cause of death?"

"Yeah, we're calling it a stabbing."

He nods. "Okay." Sitting up, he rubs his hands on his knees. I get the feeling he wants to say something, but neither my useless mood ring nor my semi-retired psychic senses offer any assistance.

He reaches out and picks up the red shard from the coffee table. "Where'd this piece of taillight come from?"

I lean forward eagerly. "You know what that is?"

"Yeah. Oh, for sure. It's a broken piece of taillight from—" he holds it up and runs his thumb along the edge as he inspects it more closely "—the right taillight. Seems like it might be an older vehicle, just based on the opacity and the diffusion texture."

I let out a low whistle. "Turns out you're pretty handy to have around. How do you know so much about cars?"

He turns the debris over in his hand as he answers. "I like patterns. I like the way cars have consistencies and the way they evolve over time. When I was real little, I thought maybe it would be something that I'd have in common with my dad. Turns out he's not really into cars. But once I started studying the patterns, I just couldn't let it go. The things that change, the style, materials, I just sort of absorbed it. You know?"

Nodding, I chew my bottom lip and reply, "I do. I think that's how it is with me and movies. There are so many tropes that repeat over and over again, but there are also subtle differences, unique interpretations. It's all swirling around in here somewhere." I tap my finger on my temple.

Reaching across the table, I open my hand and he drops the bit of crimson plastic into my out-stretched palm. As soon as the plastic touches my skin, the word "tracks" hits me like a brick wall. I see an image of a tire track in the snow. "I have to go back to your house. I think whoever took the endangered species from the taxidermy shed left some kind of tire track."

Stellen sits up and shakes his head. "We drove in and out of there a few times, and didn't you say the sheriff and the deputy drove both their cruisers down the road?"

I nod.

"Doesn't seem like you'll be able to find anything, plus it's snowed a little off and on. I bet any tracks that were left would be covered."

I jump up from the couch and grab my coat. "One thing you gotta learn, kid. When I get a hunch, it's always worth following."

"RE-OW!" Game on!

Stellen stands and scratches between Pyewacket's ears. "I better come with you. You don't know anything about tires."

"Rude. But you're not wrong."

The sun sparkles off the fresh layer of white powder blanketing almost-Canada. The bright, upbeat scenery lies in stark contrast to our mission. However, the ominous Jablonski estate does not disappoint. The weather-beaten cabin still holds every ounce of its inherent dreariness.

Rather than drive through and potentially further obscure the tracks we seek, I park in the driveway and Stellen and I hop out.

"Where did the chunk of taillight come from?" He stops at the front of the Jeep and waits for me.

"My co-investigator, Pyewacket, delivered that tidbit."

Stellen raises his eyebrows and his mouth makes a little surprised oh-shape. "Does he always help you?"

As I stop to ponder the question, it surprises me to take stock of the number of times that wildcat has saved my skin or provided key information. "Now that I think about it, yeah. He seems to be in tune with information that's somehow beyond my human perception."

Stellen nods in agreement, as though my statement is as commonplace as adding cream to coffee. "So you don't actually know where the taillight was broken, right?"

Taking a page from Pyewacket's book, I reply, "Can confirm."

He pauses in the curve of the driveway and scans the surroundings. "If it happened here . . . What would he, or she, have hit?"

As soon as my sidekick mentions a collision, my clairvoyance delivers a flash of a taillight impacting a tree. Sadly, there is no extended visual on the vehicle or the driver, just pitch blackness surrounding — "Look! Is there bark scraped off that tree?"

Stellen shifts his gaze toward a huge old pine tree whose branches are weighed down with the burden of fresh snow.

I make a beeline toward the tree, but my cohort grabs my arm. "Wait. There could be part of a track still visible under those huge branches. They would've blocked the snow from covering it. We need to take pictures, or measurements of the track, right?"

"Hey, you're a natural. We absolutely need to do all of those things. Does your dad have a measuring tape in the shed?"

The kid whips out his phone. "I've got an app for that."

We share a giggle and inch toward the scarred pine tree.

Stellen squeezes my arm in excitement. "Right there. That's a track from a BF Goodrich All-terrain T/A KO."

"I'm not even going to ask how you know that."

He shrugs. "Tread patterns. It's one of those things. But that's an older tire. It's been discontinued. Maybe that'll help the sheriff narrow down his search for the vehicle?"

He snaps a few pics and uses the app to measure width and depth of the track.

I pat him on the back. "And it will have a busted right tail light, too."

He nods. "Yeah, that scrape wasn't there before the—you know—the accident."

"It stands to reason that whoever stole the leopard, sea turtle, condor, and the tools, is the same person who hit this tree."

"Yeah, but I still don't get why they stole them. I would've handed them over, or I could've finished them if they really needed me to."

"So you're pretty good at taxidermy?"

"Not to brag, but they have the world championships every two years, and my dad's placed in the top three for the last five competitions. Three of those mounts were more than half my handiwork.

But he puts on the finishing touches, so who knows."

"I'm sure your work made a difference." An awkward silence threatens, but my spinning brain offers a different distraction. "Hey, what about the tools? When we were here the other day with Silas, you mentioned they stole some tools. Do you know which ones?"

"I can totally tell what's missing. I organized that whole tool bench for my dad. Let's go back inside and make a list."

He scans the wall behind the bench and calls out the names of the MIA tools. "Let's see, they took the shaving knife, the hone, the eye scoop, the curved spring forceps, and the broad sculpting spatula."

"Those tools all sound really specialized. Can you show me what they look like?" Taking a deep breath, I steel myself, and promise not to think about what the tools are used for.

He quickly calls up some pictures on his phone, but as he mentioned on our last visit, the internet lags and it takes some time for the pictures to load.

As he scrolls through the shots and points to the types of tools that were taken from his dad's workbench, my breath catches in my throat. "What's that one? The super long piece?"

"Oh, it's called a hone. We use it to restore the edge on other tools."

"And that was one of the things that was taken?"

"I'm pretty sure."

"Is this long part kind of strong? It's made out of metal, right?"

"It's steel. The one we had was about nine-inches long. It's important to keep after the curl on the edge of skinning tools and stuff. If the blade wilts, it affects the precision."

There's only one part of his mini-lesson that interests me. "Nine inches? You're sure?"

"Yeah, why?"

"The description of the murder weapon mentioned something with a nine-inch shank. The medical examiner hypothesized a screwdriver."

The color drains from Stellen's face. "If it was the hone . . . My dad might've been killed here, in the shop."

I scan the porous wooden floor. "I don't think so. We would've seen bloodstains on a floor like this."

The young boy steadies himself on the bench. "Not if it happened in the back." He gulps down some air and whispers, "I call it the grim reaper room."

Now it's my turn to feel queasy. "Do I even want to know what that is?"

He shakes his head. "You better call Erick, I mean Sheriff Harper."

Great. Another opportunity for me to disappoint my possibly *ex*-boyfriend.

Stellen and I make good use of our time while we wait for the deputies to arrive. We need a distraction from the thoughts swirling in our minds, so we head off to work in the house.

I'm told that it's important to leave the heat on, even though he's not living here. Setting the furnace to a low temp keeps the pipes from freezing. Next we attempt to clean out the refrigerator. There's precious little food in there to begin with, but there's no point in letting it rot and stink up the whole place. We pack three grocery bags with perishables and some dry goods from the cupboards, and Stellen grabs two framed pictures from the wall in their sparsely furnished living room.

"I hear the cars. Should we meet them outside?" His youthful face is struggling to find courage.

"You load this stuff in the Jeep. I'll talk to the deputies." As I trudge out to the taxidermy shed, I cross my fingers inside my mittens. Hopefully, it will be only deputies, and no sheriff.

No such luck.

Sheriff Harper steps out of his vehicle, taps the button on his radio, and calls in. "10-8 at the Jablonski property." His jaw muscles flex. "Dispatch said there was a call about some new evidence. This your doing?"

The harsh tone of his voice hurts my heart, but I don't feel it's unwarranted. "Do you want me to talk to Deputy Johnson?" I peer over Erick's shoulder as his backup approaches.

Erick crosses his arms over his chest in that yummy way that makes his biceps bulge, which only pains me further. "No, Miss Moon. I'd like you to tell me exactly what you found. Or is this just a hunch?"

Ouch. Handing him the shard of taillight, I walk him through our discovery of the tire track and the specific tools that were missing from the shed.

"You say this hone has a nine-inch shank?"

"Yeah, that's what Stellen said. He's the one who organizes all the tools for his dad, so he knew exactly what was missing. When he showed me the picture of the hone, I thought it could be the murder weapon?"

Erick tilts his head, and my psychic senses finally deliver a useful message. He's impressed with my deduction, and it's difficult for him to keep from telling me. He's weakening.

"If the murder weapon was taken from this location, there's a chance the murder took place here and not on the mountain."

"That means it might not be Mr. Lee. Right?"

"I'm not at liberty to discuss an ongoing investigation with a civilian."

Yeesh! "Well, there's no blood in the taxidermy shed. But Stellen mentioned something he calls 'the grim reaper room,' and I didn't want to see it."

Erick's eyes widened, and he nods slowly. "It's a terrible nickname, but it would be the location where Mr. Jablonski processed the animals before mounting them. I'll have the deputies check into it." He turns to pass instructions to Deputy Johnson and I'm left standing in the snow like an abandoned Christmas tree in January.

Stellen waves from the car. I shrug and walk toward my Jeep.

As I yank open the door in a huff, the sheriff's voice calls out across the winter landscape.

"Thanks for calling this in, Moon."

"You're welcome, Erick." Before we were an item, my using his first name really got under his skin. Maybe I can soften him up by using a few of my old tricks.

He turns away to hide his smile, but I've revealed another crack in his icy shell.

CHAPTER 13

I BARELY RECOGNIZE my own bookstore when
Stellen and I return from our investigation. Twiggy
wasted no time in getting the inventory boxed up
and moving the shelving to make way for the wedding festivities.

"Wow! This space is enormous. All those book-
cases really make it seem a lot smaller."

Twiggy stomps out, crosses her arms, and fixes
me with an impudent stare. "It's called creating a
cozy atmosphere. People appreciate that when
they're browsing for their next favorite read."

"I know I don't say it enough, but I really do appreciate everything you do for the bookshop. I'm
sorry we had to upset the apple cart to make the
bride happy, but she's my one and only father's fi-

ancée, so I kind of feel like I need to make her happy."

A mischievous sparkle twinkles in Twiggy's eye. "Just wait till you see the dress. You're going to make a whole lot of people happy." She cackles all the way back to her rolly office chair.

"Let's head upstairs. How do you feel about ordering pizza for dinner?"

Stellen grins. "I'm never gonna say no to pizza."

Chuckling, I place the call and check the apartment to see if there's any additional evidence coming in from my furry informant.

"I'm gonna give my dad a quick call. Here's some cash. Will you pay for the pizza when they get here?"

Stellen retrieves the bills from the coffee table. "I think this is too much. How much did you want to tip?"

"You decide. And keep whatever is left."

He gulps loudly. "Thanks."

"Let's call it your allowance. I'm sure there'll be plenty of opportunities for you to pitch in while we're all trying to get ready for this wedding. You'll earn it twice over before the end of the week."

He nods. "No problem. I'm happy to help."

This cooperative attitude is refreshing. Having to deal with a stubborn Ghost-ma, a curmudgeonly alchemist, and an opinionated volunteer employee has conditioned me to expect resistance at my every suggestion. This kid is a real keeper.

"Hey, Dad, I was wondering— Sure. Right now? Got it. Be right there." I end the call and update my roommate. "Save me a slice. Apparently the bride needs to speak to me right away."

Stellen smiles and his face transforms into an impish grin. "Sure. I'll save you a *slice*."

Rolling my eyes and shaking my head, I don my winter coat and hustle over to wedding central.

The elevator doors glide open, and the look on my father's face is everything.

"Um, you look a little overwhelmed. How can I help?"

As I step into the penthouse, the muffled sobs from the back bedroom are audible. I lean toward my father and whisper, "Is everything all right? Did you guys have a fight?"

He pours us each a shot of whiskey and refuses to answer until we've downed the golden-amber liquid.

He wipes the corner of his mouth with the back of his hand. "Don't tell Mom. You know how she thinks anyone who drinks under pressure is an alcoholic."

His concise summary of Isadora Duncan's Alcoholics Anonymous-based judgment brings an instant chuckle. "Don't worry. I'm constantly having to tell her how I support her struggle and am glad to know she found a path to sobriety, but that since I'm not an alcoholic, I'm allowed to have wine in the apartment."

My father smiles, but his sharp inhale indicates more to this story.

I jut my thumb toward the continued weeping. "What's going on?"

"She just got a call from her mother. Her dad was loading the suitcases into the car and suffered a heart attack. Amaryllis is pretty broken up about it. They'll know more tomorrow, but it could mean that her folks won't be able to attend the wedding."

"She's close to them?"

Jacob nods. "Yeah, they're one of those rare families that all get along and respect each other. Her father encouraged her to follow her dreams, and her mom approved of all of her decisions."

My father and I share the same startled expression before a wave of guilt washes over his features.

"Don't look like that, Dad. We both have baggage and we're doing everything we can to build a better relationship moving forward."

He refills our shot glasses. "I can't tell you what it means to me that you let me be a part of your life. I can't change the past, but I'm not gonna take a chance on messing up the future."

We clink our shot jiggers and round two goes

down the hatch. A double-tap of the empty glasses on the countertop ends the ritual.

"I'll tell you the same thing that I tell Grams. All of our choices brought us to where we are now. I'd certainly like to go back and change a few things, but what if that meant I didn't end up in Pin Cherry Harbor? That would be the true tragedy."

My father smiles at me. "And then you wouldn't have met Sheriff Harper, right?"

His comment knocks the grin right off my face. "Yeah, about that." I fill him in on the unfortunate events of Bond-marathon movie night and push my empty shooter toward the bottle.

He gives us each half a shot more and offers some advice. "I'm not going to tell you how to live your life, Mitzy, but honesty is the only thing that makes my relationship with Amaryllis work. She's a brilliant attorney and a genuinely wonderful human being. She obviously has her pick of the litter. Why she would choose an ex-con with daddy issues and an interfering ghost for a mother-in-law is beyond me. The important thing is she knows everything about me, and she chose me anyway. You're selling yourself short if you don't give Erick the same opportunity."

Maybe it's the booze, or maybe my dad is actually making some sense, but I'm starting to consider the genuine possibility of having to let my guard all the way down. "I'll take it under advisement. I'm sure you didn't call me over here to endure the tale of my sorry love life. What does she need?"

He sighs and places both hands on the black granite countertop. "She needs her father to heal miraculously and arrive on our doorstep before the wedding, but since neither of us possess that kind of mojo, I was sort of hoping you'd try on your bridesmaid's dress and look at her hairstyle photos." His voice falters at the end and he swallows loudly.

"So you called me over here to be a sacrificial lamb? Real nice, Duncan."

He smiles sheepishly. "I'll definitely owe you one, world's best daughter."

I roll my eyes dramatically for his benefit. "Oh brother." Patting him on the shoulder, I shuffle down the hallway toward an uncertain fate. I ease the door open and lower my voice as I offer myself up. "Amaryllis? I don't want to intrude, but Dad thought I might be able to—"

Her tear-streaked face turns, and she grabs a handful of tissues. After an alarmingly forceful nose blowing, she wipes her eyes and pushes her hair back from her face. "Thank you, Mitzy. I'm sure my pops will be fine, and that's the most important part. It just breaks my heart to have him miss the wedding, you know?"

I really don't, but now is not the time to discuss

my orphan-esque frame of reference and my difficulty in assimilating into family life. "I do. I was wondering if maybe you'd like to take your mind off things for a little while? Maybe I could try on the dress and you can decide what you want to do with my hair?" Fear coils around my spine as I offer these insane options.

"That's brilliant. I really appreciate the offer. It will definitely help to take my mind off things. Sitting here, crying and waiting for my phone to ring with an update is making me a nervous wreck." As she bustles into her closet, her voice carries an upbeat tone. "Let me grab the dress, and you can change in the bathroom if you're shy." She steps out with a beautiful garment bag and passes it to me.

"I'll just hop in there and get changed."

She rubs her hands together eagerly. "I can't wait to see you in it. It'll be perfect with your coloring." She leans over the bedside table and rifles through a stack of magazines. "You go change, and I'll find the pages I marked for possible hairdos. This is such fun. I'll grab a bottle of the wedding champagne and a couple glasses. No fitting is complete without bubbly! Thank you so much for coming over."

I step into the luxurious bathroom, close the door, and marvel at the classy appointments. Beautiful marble countertops, a double sink, a massive soaking tub, and a walk-in shower. My father may have temporarily turned his back on the Duncan fortune, but it seems as though he's coming back around.

Stripping off my winter layers, I toss everything to the floor. However, the pile of refuse looks out of place in such a fancy room. I'm compelled to fold all my clothes and place them in a neat stack between the sinks.

Unzipping the garment bag, I suck in a quick breath when I see the gorgeous red velvet dress. It's breathtaking. A fabulously ruched gown, with an off-the-shoulder neckline, a bow-back, and white faux-fur trim. A quick peek at the tag reveals it's a Badgley Mischka Couture creation. Ghost-ma would be thrilled. This promises to be quite the winter wonderland affair.

Removing the dress from the bag, I twirl it back and forth on the hanger. The overall look of the dress has a bit of a Victorian flair, and there's matching white faux-fur trim all around the bottom of the mermaid silhouette skirt. I unzip the dress and try it on.

The emphasis is on *try*. Because, despite the fully functioning zipper, there is no way in all of Christmastown that this dress is going to fit over my hips.

Before giving up completely, I attempt to put

the whole contraption over my head. This results in half of a success. The top half. The waistline of the gown is too narrow, and the zipper refuses to come anywhere near closing over my ample backside.

Pacing in front of the mirror, I look a bit like a holiday tree skirt gone wrong. The last thing Amaryllis needs right now is another problem, but if I don't show her the dress, she'll think I don't approve.

Tossing my pride straight into the waste bin, I open the door and attempt a bit of comedy. "Well, you were right about the color. It definitely brings out the red in my cheeks."

Amaryllis looks up from the stack of magazines she's madly leafing through. Her initial expression of disappointment quickly transforms to mirth. "Oh dear. I'm so sorry! I didn't know your size. You look like such a tiny thing. I guess I underestimated those Duncan hips."

For a split second I'm offended, but then I realize she's complimenting a trait I share with my grandmother—and she did refer to me as a "tiny thing." "I always forget that you knew Isadora. You'll have to tell me what she was like before she got sick. I'm sure you dealt with her on more than one occasion. It seems her and Cal never quite got over each other."

Amaryllis clutches her stomach and stifles a

guffaw. "Understatement of the century! Not that Isadora got over any of her ex-husbands, but she and Cal were such a pair. She definitely passed on her feisty streak. You and Jacob are a couple of tough customers."

I grab the edges of my hopelessly unzipped skirt and feign a curtsy. "I represent that remark."

We both laugh and she crosses the room to see how dire my situation truly is.

"Hmmmm." She sets down her crystal flute and taps her pearlescent fingernail on her bottom lip. Her head tilts back and forth as she surveys the catastrophe. "Try sucking in your stomach."

I oblige her request, and she tugs mercilessly on the zipper.

"It really is the hips, isn't it?"

I nod. "Unfortunately, I can't suck those in."

"No, of course not. You're perfect just the way you are. I'm the one who got the wrong size dress. There's just no time to replace it. I had to order it from a dressmaker in Chicago."

When she mentions dressmaker, I get a lovely idea. "Silas recently introduced me to a tailor in Broken Rock. Maybe he can make this work somehow."

Amaryllis throws her arms around me, and her icy hands send chills across my exposed back. "That's perfect! You take the dress home with you and get in touch with this tailor. Maybe he makes house calls. I'm sure he can figure something out. Perfect! Now that we've taken care of that, let's get down to business with this hairstyle."

Time loses all meaning as I sip champagne and watch Amaryllis page through magazine after magazine, folding corners over on a variety of hairdos that will never see the light of day on my head. Eventually my savior, I mean my dad, opens the door and offers a reprieve. "I was going to see if you girls wanted me to order— Wow, Mitzy. Is that how the dress is supposed to look?"

Crossing my arms over the velvet disaster, I narrow my gaze. "Do not test me."

His eyes widen, and he nods firmly. "Understood. Pizza, Chinese, or burgers?"

Amaryllis clutches my arm. "You decide. I'm too stressed out to think about food."

I wish I could say that I can relate to that concept in even a small way, but stress has the exact opposite effect on me. "Stellen and I have a pizza en route, but I'll call and have him bring it over. So, let's add some burgers, fries, and pin cherry pie à la mode to that, and we'll have a feast."

My father smiles and flashes his eyebrows. "That's my girl."

Amaryllis presses a hand to her chest. "Just get a cup of soup for me, Jacob. I have no appetite."

He nods, slips out of the room, and softly closes the door.

I hop off the bed and stride toward the bathroom. "No appetite. What a concept."

Her laughter follows me as I change back into my comfortable, zip-able clothes.

Stellen brings the pizza over and the four of us settle in for the evening. My dad attempts to get board games started, but Stellen and I insist on a movie marathon.

Since we're between holidays, we all agree on appropriately themed selections. We allow each person one choice.

Amaryllis chooses *Serendipity*. A solid pick.

My father goes with *Home Alone*, which technically only qualifies as a holiday movie because of the set decoration. If you ask me, it's more of a heist-gone-wrong/action film.

Stellen comes out of left field with a surprise pick of Bing Crosby's *White Christmas*.

"You've got some serious filmographic knowledge, buddy." I pat him on the back and he blushes.

"Not really. That one was my mom's favorite."

"Now it's your turn, Mitzy." My dad holds the remote firmly, poised to add my selection to the playlist.

"I have way too many favorite holiday movies to pick just one!"

"You're about to lose your right to choose. I'll give you five seconds before I give your choice to Stellen." Jacob grins and gives my sidekick a "bro" nod.

"Fine, if you're going to be an absolute Grinch—"

My dad leans forward. "Is that your pick?"

"Absolutely not. My pick is *Elf*."

Stellen pumps his fist and Amaryllis gives a little "yes" as Dad types my selection into the search bar.

As I scan the faces illuminated by the light of the large-screen TV, my heart nearly bursts. This is what family should feel like. Acceptance. Support. Shared memories.

Amaryllis doesn't even stay awake long enough to make it to her pick, and as my broad-shouldered father scoops her up from the couch, he glances at his remaining guests. "Hey, you two wanna sleepover? I'm sure I can rustle up some snacks, and maybe we can think of a few more movies for the queue. What d'you say?"

I exchange a shrug with Stellen. "We don't have any other plans. Let's do it!"

He smiles but adds, "I just have to be at the clinic by eleven. Doc Ledo's going to let me observe a C-section on a basset hound."

Tossing a pillow at him, I laugh as he ducks out

of the way. "You and I have very different ideas of entertainment, kid."

He snickers and tosses the pillow back.

I don't know how long Silas can keep Child Protective Services at bay, but I sure am enjoying my attempt to pay it forward.

CHAPTER 14

THE INSISTENT BUZZ of my cell phone yanks me out of my sorry excuse for dreamland and I reach toward the bedside table. Problem is, I'm not in my bed.

Instead of a wooden structure, my hand meets with thin air and I flop off the couch with a thud.

Stellen pops up from his pile of pillows on the floor. "Are you okay? Did you fall?"

"If there's one thing you should know about me, it's that I'm not a morning person. Now help me find my phone."

"On it."

We riffle through empty bags of chips, crisps, and crackers, but the phone is not on the coffee table.

"It's coming from your coat."

"Right!" I dive for the winter-wear-covered ottoman and dig into the pocket of my puffy jacket. "Silas. What would possess you to call at this hour?"

Unsurprisingly, he harrumphs and informs me that it is nearly nine in the morning.

"Point taken. Please continue. Stellen? Yeah, he's here. Done. Let me put it on speakerphone." I tap the speaker button and set the phone on the coffee table.

"Good morning, Mr. Jablonski. Did you sleep well?" Silas patiently awaits a response.

Stellen looks at me and scrunches up his face in confusion.

I wave my hand in a circular motion, trying to show that he has to go through the motions to get to the actual news. Somehow he understands.

"Good morning, Mr. Willoughby. I slept well. And you?"

I can almost hear Silas grinning on the other end of the phone. "A fine set of manners, young man. I apologize for disturbing you so early."

Rude. He didn't apologize for disturbing *me* so early.

"I've completed my examination of your father's estate. It pains me to report that he bore the burden of enormous debt. I'm sure you're aware of the high cost of medical bills surrounding your mother's illness."

Stellen nods. "Yeah. He complained about that a lot."

"Please do not infer this to be insensitive, but he had good reason. He had taken a second mortgage on the property and leveraged his accounts receivables to secure additional loans. In a word, your father was bankrupt."

Stellen sighs and shakes his head. "I wish he would've let me get a job. I don't think helping him with the taxidermy stuff really added anything to our bottom line."

"Perhaps we may never know the answer, but those critically endangered mounts that were stolen would have gone a long way toward pushing your father closer to being in the black."

"But we don't know who took them. What are we gonna do now?"

"Perhaps Mizithra can be of some assistance in locating them. Is it your intention for the Duncan-Moon Philanthropic Foundation to clear the Jablonski debts?"

I open my mouth to answer, but Stellen shakes his head vigorously. "No. No way. None of this is your fault. I want to sell the place. Any of the mounts that don't belong to clients, you can sell at auction, and you can list the property with a local realtor, or whatever."

My heart breaks a little, and I lean toward him. "Stellen, are you sure you want to do that? What about—your mom?"

He takes a deep breath and stares at the floor. "I have to move on. If I hang onto the house just because of the memories, what will it prove? I still want to go to veterinary school, and there's no guarantee that I would get to do my internship in Pin Cherry. I may as well sell the property now, rather than have you waste a bunch of your money trying to put out this dumpster fire of a situation."

I press my lips together firmly and nod my head. "I understand. It's your decision."

Silas clears his throat. "I shall begin the process. However, I believe it serves all of our interests to find the missing mounts."

"I agree. We'll get back to the bookshop and take another look at the murd—3 x 5 cards. You know, see if we're missing some connection."

Silas makes an odd sound. A combination between a groan and a squeak of surprise. "I was under the impression that my call had awakened you. How is it that you are not at the bookshop?"

"Oh, we're across the alley, at Dad's. I came over for some wedding stuff last night, and Dad asked me to stay for dinner. So, Stellen joined us and we had a holiday movie marathon."

Silas chuckles. "Most excellent. I shall be in touch regarding the progress of listing the property."

"Thanks. We'll check in later." I end the call and rub the sleep from my eyes.

"Let's grab our stuff and slip out. Are you all right with Fruity Puffs for breakfast?"

He grins as he places the throw pillows back on the sofa. "I prefer it."

"That's what I'm talking about."

After I drop Stellen at the animal hospital, my conscience and my mood ring stab me simultaneously. The handsome face of Sheriff Harper swirls within the black cabochon.

"Fine. Message received."

Am I ready for this? Let's see . . .

Big girl pants: check.

Heart on sleeve: check.

Terrified beyond reasonable doubt: check.

I drive to the sheriff's anyway and park on Main Street.

The station has returned to its normal, uninhabited state. The bullpen is empty, and Deputy Baird/Furious Monkeys is busily playing the app on her phone. All traces of tipsters and complainants have vanished.

"Good morning. What level are you on now?"

"I hit 225 this morning. It unlocks a whole new jungle and molten-lava-filled coconuts." Her eyes never leave the screen, but a smile briefly touches her lips.

"Nice work. Is he in?"

She nods, and if not for my extrasensory perception, I never would've noticed the concern that seeps from her aura.

Hurrying through the bullpen, I take a deep breath and step into his office.

His head whips up from the stack of papers that moments before held all of his attention. The initial smile is warm, but then he seems to remember that we're fighting. His jaw clenches and he leans back in his chair. "What brings you in, Moon?"

Taking a seat that wasn't offered, I paste on a weak smile. "I could say I'm here to get some information about the murder weapon, but that would be a lie, and I feel like our relationship is at the point where we should be honest with each other."

The tossing of his words back in his face brings an actual smile to his gorgeous full lips. "I see. So let me ask you again, why are you here?"

"May I close the door?"

The heat that races through his eyes sends my

tummy into a tingly swirl. He picks up a pen, looks around, and sets it back on the desk. "Sure. I guess."

I slowly close the door and turn the lock. I'm unable to prevent the refrain from the Kenny Rogers' song from shooting through my head, but this is no time for jokes.

Returning to my seat, I take a ragged breath. "I need to tell you something. I know I should've told you sooner, and that's on me. And I know it sounds like an excuse, but it's not. It's not that I don't trust you, it's just kind of out there, and it scared me."

The crack in my voice brings down his shields. He leans forward, walks his fingers across the desk, and turns up his palm.

Looking at his hand, I smile. "I can hold your hand in a minute, but if I touch you right now I'm going to start crying, and totally lose my nerve."

He nods. "The hand's not going anywhere. What do you need to tell me, Moon?"

"I can see ghosts."

He chews his bottom lip and nods. "So, Isadora really is haunting the bookshop?"

"I don't think she'd call it haunting. She's managing her afterlife existence, while remaining at the bookshop."

He chuckles. "That sounds like something she'd say."

My throat tightens and I wish I could stop there. "It's not just Isadora. I see other ghosts too."

He nods, but I can sense his nervousness growing. That's all I can say today. If I tell him anything else, it will be too much. No point in giving him a drink from a fire hose on day one. I'll just leave it as *Sixth Sense* as possible for now, and maybe there'll be an opportunity in the future to mention the rest of my messed-up deal.

"Was there anything else?"

I gulp down some air. "To be perfectly honest, there is. But would it be all right to focus on the seeing ghosts thing today and you stop hating me?"

Before I have a chance to exhale, he is out of his chair and rounding the desk. He reaches down, scoops me close, and snuggles his face into my hair. "I could never hate you. Never. I was hurt, and it upset me that you didn't trust me. But there was never even a split second where I hated you."

I melt into his chest and wonder how long he'll let me stay in his arms.

A bang against the door, a mumbled curse, and a firm knock, answer the question for me.

Erick pulls away slightly and turns toward the door. "Who is it?"

"Deputy Paulsen. We brought that mechanic in for questioning."

"Thank you, Deputy. I'll be right out."

She mumbles something under her breath, and I hear her little feet stomp away.

"I guess I better get out of here."

Erick gives me a crooked grin. "Not quite yet." His warm lips meet mine, and the joy of acceptance floods over me as we kiss and make up.

Erick is the first to let the real world creep back in. "I better go talk to this witness. Should I stop by later?"

Ignoring my racing heart is impossible, but I can manage to get my breathing under control before I reply. "Sure. I just have to take care of some wedding stuff for Amaryllis, and *not* forget to pick up Stellen from the animal hospital, but other than that I have zero plans."

He chuckles and lets his hands linger on my waist. "Next time, don't wait so long to admit you were wrong."

My eyebrows hike upward and my mouth hangs open in speechless awe.

He leans in and kisses me softly. "You can tell me anything, Moon. Never forget that."

Pulling myself together, I nod slowly. "I'm working on it. Please be patient during construction. We are making a better Mitzy for you."

He smooths the hair back from my face and pulls away with regret. "See you later."

"Yeah. Sounds good, Sheriff."

He chuckles as he unlocks the door.

"Oh, wait. There's one more thing."

He turns and flashes me that irresistible crooked grin. "Oh yeah? And what would that be?"

I reach out a hand to steady myself on his old metal desk and my knees go all wiggly jiggly. "Would you come to my dad's wedding with me?"

His expression turns from playful to serious in a flash. "Twiggy didn't tell you?"

"Would it surprise you to know that she tells me almost nothing?"

He shakes his head and inhales sharply. "She asked me to run security for the Rare Books Loft. Apparently it has to be open during the ceremony and reception, and she doesn't want any riffraff making it upstairs."

I pull my hand from the desk and place it firmly on my curvy hip. "She did what? She hired my boyfriend to work at my dad's wedding?"

Tilting his head, he shrugs one shoulder. "To be fair, I think she was worried you'd be too stubborn to apologize, and she was attempting to force us into the same room."

A smile breaks through my frown. "Yeah, that definitely checks out. Well, you can tell her you're no longer working the wedding, since—"

He interrupts my rant with a muscular arm

around my waist. "Because I'm working something else?"

My knees threaten to abandon me. "Because you are officially attending as my plus one." My voice goes up at least an octave and my eyelids are fluttering spastically.

He laughs heartily and exits the office.

I take a deep breath, smooth my hair, and walk out as though I wasn't just making out with the sheriff in his office.

Sadly, my acting isn't that great.

All heads turn in the bullpen, and deputies Johnson and Gilbert exchange unnecessary smirks.

Hustling out of the station, I jump into the Jeep and call Mr. Gustafson.

"Hello, it's Mitzy Moon."

He gushes about how wonderful it was to meet Isadora's granddaughter, and asks a series of rapid-fire questions about the suit, which I cannot answer.

"Actually, I was kind of hoping you might make a house call. I have a bridesmaid's dress that urgently needs to be altered, but I just don't have time to drive to Broken Rock this afternoon. I have to pick up my ward from his apprenticeship."

As he checks his day planner and mumbles various options, I chuckle inwardly at the grouping of words that just came out of my mouth. I really do sound a little like Bruce Wayne.

"Two o'clock? That would be perfect. And no pressure, but I'm going to need a miracle."

His laughter is light and airy, and he assures me he's never met an alteration he can't master.

Poor man. The hips of Mitzy Moon may be the end of his winning streak.

CHAPTER 15

Cut to —

"So, Mr. Gustafson took a million measurements and scooped the dress into his arms as though he was cradling a newborn babe, and assured me he'd have the dress back in my hands in time for the wedding."

Amaryllis wipes a hand across her brow and exhales loudly. "Whew, that is a load off my plate. Thank you so much for handling that. In fact, you're doing so wonderfully, I was hoping you might stop by the patisserie and make a couple of changes to my cake order."

This maid of honor gig is way harder than I anticipated. "Sure. No problem." Maybe I should make a recording on my phone with this patented answer that seems to fall out of my mouth every time my almost-stepmother makes a request.

"Oh, I almost forgot, Jacob and I wanted to talk to you about something." She presses her hands to her mouth and squeezes her shoulders up in excitement.

For some reason my mood ring tingles briefly, but no image appears. A sense of unease settles over me, and I sincerely hope she's not about to tell me she's pregnant. Not that I have anything against her and my father having a family, but they will probably ask me to babysit, and I'm absolutely the worst with screaming infants. "Sure. No problem."

She ushers me to the living room and calls for Jacob to join us.

They snuggle together on the loveseat, and I fiddle with the zipper pull on one of her many throw pillows, as I struggle to find a comfortable position on the sofa.

"Your father and I have been talking." She gazes lovingly at my dad and he grips her small hand in his large one and gives it a gentle squeeze.

"By the way, I promise I wasn't eavesdropping, I was just coming out to make coffee, and I overheard."

My mind is racing, and I have no idea what she's talking about.

My father picks up the baton. "Amaryllis and I

would like to buy the Jablonski property. I think we can convert it into a unique halfway house, and possibly a career-retraining center. Regardless, I know we can make great use of the property to support the restorative justice program."

"Oh, well, that's great. Silas will be thrilled to learn that he sold the property before he even listed it."

They chuckle uncomfortably and exchange an unreadable glance.

"Why are you two so nervous? There's more isn't there?"

Amaryllis nods. "I want you to know that we would never dream of replacing you. You're Jacob's one-and-only daughter, and you're the second most important person in my life right now. I'm so looking forward to all of us being a family."

On the surface her comment seems positive, but why are the hairs on the back of my neck standing on end. "Yeah, I'm looking forward to us being a family too. I'm still waiting for the other shoe to drop, though."

My father chews his bottom lip, fidgets in his seat, and swallows audibly. "Everything Amaryllis said is exactly how I feel. Having you in my life and building our relationship is very important to me. I don't want you to think of this as anything that will take away from our bond."

I can't take it anymore. I toss the pillow onto the sofa next to me and lean forward. "Look, if you guys are having a baby, I'll deal with it. I'm not great with kids, but I'll figure out a way to get better. I'm not against having a halfling, or whatever, in our lives. But spill it. The suspense is killing me!"

Amaryllis throws one hand over her mouth and the other over her abdomen. My dad's mouth moves in a variety of interesting ways, but makes no audible sound.

Shrugging my shoulders, I lean back and wait for them to fill in the blanks.

She slowly peels her fingers away from her mouth and smiles. "I actually had a series of fibrous cysts removed when I was in my late twenties. I'm unable to have children of my own."

My face flushes a hideous shade of crimson. "I'm so sorry. That was so insensitive. The tension just got to me. Whatever your news is, I promise I'm happy about it."

Jacob slips an arm around her shoulders and smiles. "I'm glad to hear that, because we've decided to adopt Stellen."

Tears burst out of my eyes before I can say a single word.

Amaryllis lurches forward in a panic. "Oh dear, don't be upset, Mitzy. We promise it won't—"

I wave my hands frantically. "No. No. I'm not

upset. These are happy tears. I was so worried about what would happen to him when the temporary custody ended. What kind of foster family he'd end up with? He's such a good kid, and he's had such a tough life. I just wanted him to catch a break, you know?"

Jacob and Amaryllis nod in unison. "That's exactly how we felt. We know he graduates in the spring, but we really want to make him a part of our family, and pay for his college, and whatever he needs."

All three of us are crying now. Even my stoic father has to wipe an errant tear from his square jaw.

"All right. Now that that's settled, I'm going to go pick up my brother from his job, and maybe we can all go out to dinner to celebrate?"

Amaryllis beams and my father bobs his head in support. "That's a great idea, Mitzy. Once again, world's best daughter."

As I step into the elevator, I suddenly remember that I already made plans with Erick. "Can Erick come? I'm not trying to be weird, but we just kinda made up today, and I was supposed to get together with him tonight—"

My dad's firm hand stops the elevator door from closing, and he grins. "We did say it was a family dinner, didn't we?"

My skin turns an unbecoming shade of red for the second time. "Easy, Dad. We're barely making it work as boyfriend/girlfriend. Let's not get the donkey ahead of the cart, or is it the cart ahead of the donkey?"

He pulls his hand away and his laughter is the last thing I hear as the doors press closed.

Despite being able to keep my psychic powers a secret, I'm actually kind of terrible at keeping my mouth shut about surprises. It's going to take every ounce of willpower I don't possess to keep me from blurting out the adoption news to Stellen. The best thing I can do is to get him talking about his day at work. Maybe then I'll never have a chance to accidentally spill the beans.

"Hey, little— Stellen." Strike one.

He hops in the Jeep and tosses me a teasing side-eye. "I'm almost as tall as you. I don't think you should refer to me as little Stellen."

My forced laughter hurts my own ears. "Yeah, right? How was your day?"

The entire drive home is occupied with detailed explanations of canine C-sections and newborn basset hounds. It's not exactly my cup of tea, but it absolutely keeps me from making any more slip-ups.

"We're going out to dinner tonight. So I don't know if you need a shower or anything. I kind of had conflicting engagements, so I scooped them all together."

He tilts his head. "Wait, did you and Erick make up?"

"Wow. That's some solid reading between the lines, bro." I'm counting that as strike two, even though he thinks I'm using "bro" as if I'm a cool kid.

"Sweet. I'll get changed and hang out with Pyewacket until dinner."

"Cool. I'll find Grams and have her pick out my outfit. She lives for that."

Stellen coughs and nearly chokes. "Good one."

I furrow my brow and stare at him for a moment. "Oh, right. Because she's dead. I wish I could say I meant it that way."

He heads off to take care of personal hygiene, and I hike up to the third floor of the printing museum.

Grams is trailing the ethereal fingers of one hand down Pyewacket's back and with the other she's fanning herself with a piece of paper.

"I didn't know ghosts got hot flashes. Everything all right?"

Her sparkling eyes drift lazily across the room and she grins stupidly. "I got a response to one of my query letters."

"By the way you're fanning yourself, I'd have to say it's not a rejection."

She drops the page, and it floats lazily toward the desk's surface. She zips over to me and she's positively glowing. "It's not. They want to see the first three chapters." Her glow sputters and she collapses into horizontal repose.

"That's good, isn't it? Why are you draping yourself across an invisible fainting couch?"

She sighs heavily and clutches her pearls. "They want something called a PDF. I've written everything longhand. I've written it all longhand, with a quill pen!" She rockets up to the ceiling and swirls around in a tizzy.

"Calm down, Emily Brontë. I'm sure Stellen can type it up in no time. He probably learned how to make PDF files when he was six. We'll get it handled, don't worry."

She throws glimmering limbs around me, and her energy pulses with gratitude. "I don't know what I'd do without you, Mitzy. You're absolutely amazing."

"Careful, I may get full of myself, like some of my relatives."

She pulls back with a squeak. "Why you little—"

I turn tail and run down the stairs, taking them two at a time. For your information, it is impossible to outrun a ghost.

By the time I hit the first floor, she's already

waiting for me with a bejeweled fist on each hip. "What's your plan now, smarty-pants?"

The fear in my eyes vanishes as I realize I hold the trump card. "If you promise to let this simmer until after the wedding, I'll tell you an enormous secret."

She practically drools. "You have yourself a deal, sweetie. Now, dish."

"Jacob and Amaryllis are going to adopt Stellen."

Her mouth moves, but the sound that reaches my ears is not her voice.

"They are? For reals?"

Strike three! I'm out.

I rush forward, and Ghost-ma spins on her axis. "Stellen!" We shout in unison.

He steps toward us. "Are you serious? Did they say that? That exact thing?"

I cover my face with my hand and flail my head in shame. "Can you at least pretend to be surprised at dinner? I'm sure I wasn't supposed to let the cat out of the bag."

"Ree-OW!" A warning punctuated by a threat.

The three of us share a good long laugh.

Stellen crouches and scratches between Pyewacket's tufted ears. "Don't worry, I won't let anyone put you in a bag." He looks up at me. "Did they mean like to just foster me, or were they legally going to adopt me?"

"They said adopt. But if you don't want them to—"

He rockets to his feet. "No. I do. It's just— So, you'll be my sister?"

"Big sister."

He smiles. "That's pretty lit."

"Show me your surprised face, little brother."

He widens his eyes and lets his jaw drop open foolishly.

Grams and I have a giggle fit. "That's next level. Let's dial it back about fifteen percent at dinner, and I think we can fool everyone."

"No problem, *sis*."

I roll my eyes. "Great. The list of my tormentors grows."

Grams and I head up to the apartment to fight over wardrobe, and Pyewacket curls up on one of the oak reading tables next to Stellen and an enormous reference book.

Unless my eyes deceive me, Stellen is studying feline anatomy, and Pyewacket is actually letting the boy stretch out his powerful cat-limbs and feel the joints and ligament attachment points. I must be dreaming.

Dinner goes off without a hitch, and Stellen's impressive performance wins the night.

Erick offers me a ride back to the bookshop. Jacob and Amaryllis invite Stellen to ride with them, so they can get better acquainted and discuss how he'd like to furnish his new room.

All is quiet back at the Bell, Book & Candle, and Erick and I take advantage of the alone time. We're rather busy canoodling on the couch when Grams bursts through the bookcase wall to announce she can't find Pyewacket.

I jump backward and embarrassment floods over me.

Erick sits very still and narrows his gaze. "Anything you'd like to tell me, Moon?"

"Yes. Yes, there is." I stand and walk toward the spot where Grams is hovering.

"Myrtle Isadora Johnson Linder Duncan Willamet Rogers, I'd like you to meet my boyfriend."

She curtsies and gushes about how wonderful he is. Thankfully, he can't see or hear any of that.

"She says it's nice to meet you." I gesture for him to walk toward me, and he steps forward with considerable trepidation coursing through his veins.

As he gets closer, I see the ghost-chills raise the flesh on his arms in tiny bumps.

"Do you feel that chill?"

He nods robotically.

"That's her." I wave my arm in a grandiose arc. "Erick Harper, please meet Ghost-ma."

He chuckles in spite of the tension. "Ghost-ma. That's clever."

"Thanks, I try."

"Nice to meet your ghost, Isadora." He offers a hand and Grams unwittingly grabs it and pumps out an over-eager greeting.

Erick jumps back and shakes his hand as though a rattler bit him. "Whoa! That's going to take some getting used to. Maybe warn me next time, okay?"

Grams prattles on about how he'll get used to it if he spends more time . . . blah, blah, blah.

I choose not to translate any of the rant. "Now that we're all acquainted, I'm sure you can see we were busy, Grams."

She vanishes in a huff, but the mood is lost.

The whole exchange proves too much for my virgin-to-the-paranormal boyfriend.

Erick retrieves his coat and runs a hand through his lovely loose blond bangs. "I better head out. I've got three more witnesses to question tomorrow, and two deputies combing through vehicle registration records for 1972 to 1985 truck models. Not to mention the long list of tire sales receipts. I'm anxious to see if any of those purchases match up with the trucks. If the taillight and the tires are connected to the same vehicle, that should point us toward the person or persons who broke into the taxidermy shed."

"Do you think there's a connection? Between Jablonski's murder and the theft?"

"Right now, we're treating them as separate crimes. Mr. Lee's fingerprints were all over that screwdriver the deputies located on the mountain, but it was from his toolbox. It stands to reason that the attacker would've worn gloves, so we'll need more to secure a case against him. But once we find out who's responsible for the theft, we may adjust our theory and our list of suspects."

"I don't have any wedding duties tomorrow, so hopefully I can lend a hand in the investigation?" I hate that my question comes out as more of a plea than a statement.

He slips an arm around my waist and pulls me close. "Can she hear me if I whisper? Nod once for yes and cough for no."

I clear my throat with a short cough. Even though I can't see her, she's probably eavesdropping, but he doesn't need to know that.

"Glad you're back on my team, Moon. I'm better at my job when you're around." He kisses my cheek softly, and as he pulls his lips away, my skin misses the warmth of his touch.

Grams pops into my visible spectrum and swirls

up toward the ceiling. "I heard nothing. I saw nothing."

Her lies release an uncontrollable giggle-gulp in my throat.

Erick arches an eyebrow in concern.

"Don't worry, it's the ghost comedian, not you."

He shakes his head. "One day at a time, right? Don't get me wrong, I'm happy to be in the know, but I'm still a little unsettled to be in the inner circle."

I bat my eyelashes and grin. "We're happy to help you get settled."

My extrasensory perceptions catch a flash of desire, but he does the right thing and walks out of my apartment.

That man is too good for his own good.

CHAPTER 16

WHEN THE DOORBELL sounds announcing a visitor at the alleyway door, my heart skips a beat. I roll out of bed, shove my feet into my slippers, and throw a blanket around my shoulders, because I have no idea what I've done with my robe.

Turning off the alarm, I press one hand to the door and call out, "Erick? Is that you?"

The amused snicker of my new little brother deflates my expectations. "It's just me, Mitzy, and a half-frozen feline."

I shove the door open and Pyewacket stumbles through, followed by Stellen.

"Pyewacket, what were you doing outside? This is the serious heart of winter, son."

He turns his head, and his mouth opens, but he doesn't issue his usual snarky admonishing.

"Hey, what's wrong?" I kneel next to my fur baby and hear his rough breathing. "He's not breathing right. Should we take him to Doc Ledo?"

Stellen dives to my aid, running his hands over the cat and pressing his ear close to the caracal's chest. "There's a bloody discharge coming from his nose and his breathing is labored."

Despite his condition, Pyewacket struggles to groan.

Continuing his examination, Stellen announces, "There's something lodged in his throat."

My chest constricts, and I blink hard to fight back the tears. "I'll get the Jeep. You get a blanket."

He grips my arm. "I don't think there's time."

I gasp and press a hand to my mouth.

He gently strokes Pyewacket's fur and whispers, "I can help you, buddy. Please don't bite me."

By way of agreement, Pyewacket lays his head back and closes his eyes.

Stellen expertly traces the feline's esophagus, places a thumb in between his molars, and holds the dangerous jaw open wide. He reaches one finger in and carefully scoops deep into the animal's throat.

To Pyewacket's credit, he coughs and chokes, but he does not snap his dangerous fangs closed on his rescuer's hand.

Stellen slowly withdraws the finger and then grips something between the forefinger and thumb.

He extracts the item so delicately I forget he's a six-teen-year-old apprentice, and not a fully licensed vet.

He stares at the object and looks up at me in wonderment. "It's a key. I think it's the key to my dad's desk."

I exhale the breath I didn't realize I was hold-ing. "Put it in your pocket, and wrap this around Pye." Pulling the blanket from my shoulders, I toss it at him. "Give me two minutes to change and we're taking him to the hospital."

He nods in agreement. "Absolutely. Doc Ledo will need to make sure there's no serious damage to the esophagus."

I race upstairs with a speed that would make Usain Bolt jealous, whipping off my flannel pa-jamas as I go. In less than two minutes, I'm back downstairs fully dressed, keys in hand. "Let's hit it."

Stellen is already cradling Pye in his arms.

We hurry to the Jeep and I break all land-speed records as I race to the animal hospital.

Doc Ledo is manning the front desk, and when he sees Stellen rush in with a furry blanket-wrapped bundle, he rolls his wheelchair away from the counter and heads to one of the surgical rooms.

Stellen sounds like every paramedic on every hospital drama I've ever watched as he calls out vital statistics to the doctor as we hurry into the room.

He places my precious Pye on the table while Doc Ledo flips on lights and unwraps his instruments.

"You're sure you successfully removed the obstruction?"

"Yes, sir. I performed a finger sweep and removed it slowly to prevent any additional tissue damage."

"Good work." Doc Ledo gently strokes Pyewacket's head. "Look, buddy, you gotta be more careful with your lives. I think this brings your count down to five. I'm going to put you under, so I can run this scope down your throat. You won't feel a thing, and I promise to send you home by the end of the day."

Pyewacket slowly blinks his eyes, and even the casual observer would have to admit he understands what the doctor is telling him.

Ledo makes the injection and waits a moment for the sedative to kick in before passing instructions to his assistant.

"Turn on the monitor and hold the jaw securely while I feed the camera."

"Yes, sir."

Doc Ledo carefully threads the tiny camera down Pyewacket's throat and three pairs of eyes lock onto the monitor as we observe the key's damage.

"Was it a standard key?"

Stellen reaches into his pocket and shows the doctor. "It's more of a small skeleton key. I think it's the key to my dad's desk."

Doc Ledo finishes his examination of the esophagus and carefully retracts the camera. "Looks like superficial scratches, resulting in the blood you observed dried around the nasal cavity. No punctures. No serious lacerations." He lays the camera on a piece of blue surgical paper and removes his gloves.

Stellen closes Pyewacket's mouth and strokes his head.

"Excellent job, Stellen. That was quick thinking. You're going to make a wonderful veterinarian."

I step forward and stroke the soft fur under Pyewacket's chin. "Don't you ever scare me like that again, do you hear me, Robin Pyewacket Goodfellow?"

Stellen slips the key back in his pocket and gives me a minute with my furry companion.

He and Doc Ledo confer quietly on the far side of the surgical suite.

"What time should I come back to pick him up, Doc?"

He runs his finger down the chart and checks his watch. "We're open until 6:00 today. Why don't you come back just before closing? That'll give us time to let the sedative wear off and observe him for any difficulties eating or drinking."

"Take good care of him, all right, Stellen?"

"Hey, do you mind if we run out to my place real quick?"

"Sure, we can head out there. I'll bring you back after that errand and some breakfast. Sound good?"

He nods and checks out with Doc Ledo.

On the drive out to the Jablonski place, my mood ring sends an icy alert circling around my finger. An image of the key swirls within the black mists. "Is that key to the desk in the taxidermy shed?"

Stellen shakes his head. "No. That's what makes me suspicious. It's the key to the desk in his room. I don't even know where he kept it. Pyewacket would've had to get all the way out to the property somehow. I'll check the pads of his feet for frostbite when I get back to the clinic."

"If he took that big a risk to get the key, it has to be important. I've never known Pye to bring me useless clues."

He rubs the key between his thumb and forefinger and his gaze trails out the window. As we pull down the driveway, fresh police tape cordons off the area under the tree and the entrance to the taxidermy shed. The house looks to be fair game.

"I'll leave the car running, since this is just a quick trip. At least we'll have somewhere to warm up."

He nods and we head into the house.

Only one of the drawers on the desk is locked. Stellen employs the key, and we search through the contents together. Three folders containing birth certificates, a marriage certificate, a death certificate, and other important papers are the first things we encounter. But at the bottom of the drawer lies a journal.

Stellen pulls it out and runs his finger over the monogram. "Here. I don't think I can—"

"Understood." I take the journal and hold it in both hands. "Are you sure you want me to read it?"

He stands and walks toward the door. "I'm gonna go to the taxi shed and— I mean, maybe I'll just wait in the car. Go ahead and read some stuff, but I don't think I want to know."

"All right. If you change your mind, I'm happy to tell you what I find, or you might decide to read it yourself."

He shakes his head and hurries out of the house.

Any true fan of film and television knows that the important stuff is always written on the last few pages. While my curiosity yearns to devour the entire journal cover to cover, I'm hoping to find something useful in Mr. Jablonski's final entry.

Shockingly this movie trope does not disappoint.

And, BONUS! A folded piece of paper flutters toward the floor when I flip to the last page.

Retrieving the item, I gasp. "The page from the ledger!" Unfolding the sheet, I scan it carefully. No surprises . . . except—

A doodle in the margin catches my eye. "I wish he knew how much I missed you, Cryssie."

The thief didn't take the page to cover his or her tracks, Mr. Jablonski tore it out and secreted it away to hide his pain from his only son.

Tucking the page into the back of the journal, I hope that someday Stellen will feel safe enough to read these entries and come to a better understanding of his father's battle with love and duty. For now, I'll peruse this last entry to see if there is anything pertinent to the investigation.

December 25th

The holidays are always the hardest. I miss Crystal more than the boy will ever know. I'm doing my best to provide for him. Every day is such a struggle. I had hoped my work on the educational mounts of the endangered species would provide a means to send him to college, but today's discovery is just another nail in my coffin.

A chill runs down my spine as the eerie truth of his prediction rings in my head.

When I was going through the paperwork from the client, I noticed the same faint ink smudge on every one of the signatures from the U.S. Fish and Wildlife approval letters. Forgeries. Every one of 'em. These people are dealing in black-market animal trafficking, and now they pulled me into their web. I'll take the evidence to the sheriff tomorrow after the snocross, but there's almost no chance I come out of this unscathed. Just another way for me to let the boy down. He deserves better.

Letting the journal flop closed, I exhale sharply and get to my feet. This journal entry clearly points a finger at the traffickers and possibly takes Mr. Lee off the suspect list. I have to tell Stellen about this. He's the only one who might remember anything about the people that brought in those jobs.

"Is my boy all right?"

I'm not gonna lie, despite my now extensive experience with afterlife entities, I pee a little.

As I gaze at the floating apparition in the doorway, the brown curls and the loving green eyes are unmistakable. "Crystal?"

She surges toward me. "You can see me?"

I offer a tentative smile. "And hear you. You're Stellen's mom, right?"

Her aura glows like that of an angel, and she sighs with relief. "You know Stellen? I haven't seen him in the house for several days. I was so worried."

Since I find myself in a good news/bad news situation, I opt to start with the good news. "He's totally safe. He's been staying with me and I got him a job at the animal hospital with Doc Ledo."

"Oh, that's fantastic. I just hope Stanley can find a way to pay for college. I know he's been struggling with that."

"Crystal, I have some bad news too."

Her energy darkens as though someone is turning down the wick in an old-fashioned oil lamp. "Is it about Stanley? He's so hard on that boy. Did they have a fight? Is that why Stellen is staying with you?" She floats closer and stares at me with intense motherly concern. "Who are you?"

"First of all, let me introduce myself. I'm Mitzy Moon, Isadora Duncan's granddaughter. I inherited the bookshop on Main Street."

"Oh, I didn't know Isadora very well, only by reputation. She was a bit of a firebrand, if I remember correctly."

Covering my mouth with one hand, I chuckle. "That is accurate."

"But why is Stellen staying with you?"

"That's the bad news bit. Mr. Jablonski was murdered Friday night."

Her green eyes shift to darkest black and a serious avenging angel vibe fills the room. "Murdered? My Stanley? Who would do such a thing?"

"Take it easy, Crystal. We're investigating it. I lost my mom when I was young and I had to suffer through a series of mostly terrible foster homes, so when I heard the news about Stan, I came out here to offer Stellen a safe haven."

Her dark cloud immediately shifts to a warmer hue. "Thank you. But what happens now? He's all alone in the world . . . My sweet baby."

"The sheriff and I are investigating the murder, but in the meantime my father has offered to adopt Stellen and pay for his schooling."

I instantly recognize the sparkle of phantom tears as she clutches her chest and smiles. "Veterinary school? He's going to be a veterinarian?"

"If you ask me, he already is. He saved my caracal's life just this morning." She swirls around with the joy of a carousel horse and smiles at me with so much love it nearly breaks my heart. "Oh, my stellar Stellen! I always knew he was special. It broke my heart to have to leave before I got to see him grow up."

"Well, you did everything right, Crystal. He's a kind, thoughtful, generous boy, with a great sense of humor. My father and his new wife will take great care of him, and I promise you, I'll never let anything bad happen to him."

The apparition flickers, and a warm glow spreads out from her heart. "What's happening? I feel—"

Not that I'm an expert, but I've got more experience than your average human. "I think you're crossing over, Crystal. I think your love for Stellen and your powerful bond of responsibility kept you here."

The sparkles are growing more transparent. "Stanley was so broken after I passed away. As the cancer consumed me, I could see him losing a little more of himself each day. I just couldn't leave Stellen alone. He needed a mother's love."

"And you gave it to him. He told me about you. It was your visits that got him through the darkest days. But it's time for you to release your hold. To let him go, and for you to find the happiness you deserve on the other side of the veil."

She's barely more than a golden haze, and her voice echoes from the ether. "You'll tell him I love him? Can you keep him safe?"

"Absolutely. Rest in peace, Crystal."

And she's gone.

The silence in the room is heavy and final. Part of me feels relief that she's no longer trapped between the worlds, but a little part of me feels sadness for Stellen—that he won't see her again.

Tucking the journal under my arm, I wipe my tears and march downstairs to share the wonderful news with my ward.

A foul frigid wind has picked up speed while I was indoors, and as soon as I open the front door, loose snow swirls violently around me, obscuring my vision.

Ducking my head, and pulling my coat tight around my neck, I run for the Jeep.

And I keep running.

And as the gust of wind abates, I turn 360 degrees and stop in a trance of confusion.

"Where's the Jeep?"

CHAPTER 17

THE RING ON MY LEFT HAND BURNS, but I'm in no mood to risk frostbite and take off my mitten. No need. A clairvoyant mini-movie impacts me like a giant snowball.

The hairs on the back of my neck tingle. I see a large black SUV. It stops in front of the taxidermy shed, but the occupants must see the police tape. They stomp on the accelerator and spray a rooster tail of snow as they spin the vehicle around and tear back down the driveway.

Unfortunately, the commotion grabbed Stellen's attention, and he hopped in the driver's seat of my vehicle and gave chase.

Perfect! Not more than thirty seconds ago I promised his mother's ghost that I would take care of him and that nothing bad would happen, and now he's in pursuit of some suspected murderers!

Pulling out my phone, I dial the sheriff's station. "Please put me through to Sheriff Harper. It's urgent!"

The next voice I hear is Erick's, and I relay the events as though I witnessed them firsthand rather than psychically.

He promises to head out to the property immediately and wants me to wait inside where it's warmer.

"Copy that."

I end the call and instantly disobey his orders.

First stop the wounded pine tree. I risk pulling off my mitten and lay my hand against the scar, in hopes of a message. Unfortunately, the worry over Stellen's safety has flipped my powers into the off position.

Fine. Sheriff Harper wins. I'll wait inside.

Maybe I better call Silas and see if he has any ideas.

I re-enter the Jablonski home, lay my phone on the kitchen counter, and place the call via speakerphone, while I brew some coffee.

"Good morning, Mizithra. How may I be of assistance?"

"I've already called the sheriff, but Stellen took my Jeep and is in pursuit of possibly the murderer and maybe an illegal animal trafficker. Assuming they're one and the same."

Silas harrumphs. "That young man is too industrious. I must say, I do hope he's unsuccessful."

"What? You're wishing him ill?"

"Not at all. I am simply of the mind that catching his quarry would be the worst outcome."

"Oh, I agree." I sip my java and ponder. "What should we do?"

"I am perusing a new title that Twiggy acquired. It is extremely enlightening. I may temporarily shelve it next to *Saducismus Triumphatus*, while I complete my research. Does that suit you?"

"Sure. I don't care where you put the book, Silas. What are we going to do about Stellen?"

Holding the warm mug of coffee in both hands, to soak up as much heat as possible, I take another gulp as I wait for Silas to reply.

A second call beeps in. "Erick is calling. I've got to go."

Without waiting for Silas to acknowledge, I end his call and accept Erick's. "It's Mitzy. What's wrong?"

"In the grand scheme of things, I have to say it's more right than wrong."

"There's no time for riddles, Harper. What's going on?"

"Stellen lost control of the vehicle and slid off

the road by that dilapidated silo. He's fine. Your
Jeep is fine. But whoever was in the late model Escalade got away."

I breathe a huge sigh of relief. "Is there
more?"

Erick chuckles. "Is that a hunch?"

"Seriously!" I nearly spill my coffee as I make
an impatient gesticulation.

"Yeah, there's more. He followed them long
enough to get a license plate. I have Deputy Gilbert
on that, and Johnson is on his way out with the tow
truck. Stellen's with me, and we're coming to pick
you up."

"That's a relief."

Ending the call, I gulp down a little more coffee
and wash out the mug. I know Crystal crossed over,
but it feels wrong to leave a dirty dish in such a kind
woman's home.

Peering out the front window, I see the cruiser
rolling down the drive. I run outside and hop in the
passenger seat. Stellen's in the back, and I take advantage of the situation. "Did you arrest him for
joyriding, Sheriff?"

Stellen squeaks out a protest.

Erick laughs. "Not at all. I deputized him."

"Rude." I click my tongue and cross my arms.

Stellen leans forward and grips his fingers
through the grate dividing the rear of the vehicle

from the front. "Do you think those were the murderers?"

Erick chews his lip, deep in thought, so I field the question.

"I think they're connected to the animal trafficking. I know you said you didn't want to read your dad's journal, but I think you'll want to know that he figured out the U.S. Fish and Wildlife Service letters were forged. Whoever hired him to mount those critically endangered species was definitely running a black-market operation. He was going to bring the evidence to the sheriff, but died before he had a chance. Maybe they killed him, but I don't think they stole the mounts. If they did, they'd have no reason to come back. Right?"

Erick nods and rubs a thumb along his jaw. "Makes sense. If they killed Stan and stole the mounts, why return to the scene of the crime?"

Stellen's fingers slip out of the grating and he leans back. "It wasn't the same vehicle. That Escalade was a 2020 model and had current year tires. The taillight and the track by the tree—that's from an older truck. I'm certain."

Harper taps his thumb on the steering wheel. "As soon as Gilbert runs those plates, we'll bring 'em in. For now, let me get the two of you safely back to the bookshop. Johnson will have the tow truck drop your Jeep off in no time."

He stops the cruiser by the front of the store.

I hop out with the journal and open the rear door for Stellen. "Erick, this is Stan's journal. The last entry mentions the traffickers and there's a page from his ledger folded up in the back that shows the details of the jobs. I think we'd like the journal back though. Can you make sure nothing happens to it?"

Erick respectfully takes the journal, ducks down, and looks at Stellen. "I'll make sure that we only use what's necessary to shut these traffickers down. You have my word."

Stellen nods stiffly, and we step into the bookshop as the sheriff drives away.

The interior of the store is a flurry of activity, but it isn't the wedding preparation that catches my attention.

"I told you once, kid. She ain't here." Twiggy's voice carries the weight of authority with a sharp edge.

"Look, biker chick, I have to talk to Mitzy. She'll know what to do."

Before Twiggy can body slam our visitor, I round the corner and wave my hands as though they're white flags. "Take it down a notch, everyone. I'm here. How can I help?"

Bristol spins toward me, her face a mask of concern and admiration.

Twiggy sniffs, shakes her grey pixie cut, and stomps into the back room.

"Mitzy! Who's the old bag? I was trying to tell her how important—"

Eager to protect this girl from Twiggy's wrath. I hasten to change the subject. "Let's not rehash it, Bristol. I'm here now. Did you need something?"

Stellen leans in and whispers, "I'll see if Twiggy can take me to the clinic."

"Good idea. I'll pick you and Pyewacket up later."

Bristol's mouth tightens into a fine line, and her eyes widen. "Is Pyewacket okay? He's part of the team, right? Will you even be able to solve this case without him?"

Ignoring her boisterous fangirl rant, I attempt to drag her back on track. "Is there something I can do for you?"

"Yeah. Right. Crank didn't think I should tell you, but we haven't seen Eli since Saturday morning. He was acting super bajiggity at the race, and then he ghosted us."

It pleases me that I know bajiggity means nervous, upset, and anxious. I dive right in. "What kind of vehicle does he drive?"

She scrunches up her mouth and shrugs. "Some old '79 truck. I don't know. We call it the POC on wheels."

"And which one of you overheard coach Jablonski tendering his resignation from the Trey Lee team?"

She flicks the stud in her tongue back and forth over her lower teeth and her eyes dart up and to the left. "Well, I think AJ is the one who told Crank, and then Crank told me, but he didn't want me to tell you. But I told him that if you were gonna solve the case, you needed help—"

"So AJ overheard the conversation?"

"Maybe. Him and Eli are tight. Like, it's the four of us, but it's the two of them and then the four of us."

"So maybe Eli overheard the conversation?"

"Sure. Could be."

I slide my phone out and tap Erick's number as I toss her one more question. "And where does Eli live?"

She gives me the address, and as soon as Erick gets on the phone I fill him in. "I think if you check vehicle registration you'll find that Eli McGrail drives a 1979 Ford pickup. And if you send a deputy over to his address at County Road 13 Box number 425, you'll also find that truck has a broken taillight. And more than likely there will be some critically endangered species mounts stashed in his garage."

Erick sighs loudly and comments about my uncanny hunches before he ends the call to follow up on my lead.

"Bristol, if Coach Jablonski switched to team Priest, what would that mean for Eli?"

"Um, like, Eli is the number three seed, you know? So even though he doesn't win, he podiums at almost every race and makes some decent coin. Know what I mean?"

"I think I do. But what would happen if Freddy Priest got a coach like Jawbone?"

"Pretty likely that he'd jump from number four seed to at least number two in a couple of races. Jawbone was just that good. A magician."

"So that would push Eli off the podium, most likely permanently, right?"

"For sure. Plus Eli's hella moody. Once he starts losing, he gets super down. He might even drop out of the top ten. He'd lose his sponsors . . . It'd be major."

"Thanks, Bristol. You did the right thing by coming to me. I'll let Twiggy know, and thanks for the information."

She bobs her head and the little pom-poms at the end of the arms of her jester hat bounce up and down. "No doubt. No doubt. So, you think you got this one figured?"

I nod my head sadly. "Unfortunately, I think so."

"Sweet. I'll head out and let you wrap things up, you know?" She bows her head a couple more times. "If it's not too much trouble, like, can you mention to the paper, or whatever, how I helped?"

"If anyone asks to interview me, I will absolutely mention your help."

"Sweet. I'll put that in the blog."

"Great. Well, I better get going. I've got some stuff to finish before I pick up Pyewacket."

She stops in her tracks and turns. "Oh, right. Is he gonna be okay? Was he, like, hurt in the line of duty?"

It takes a powerful amount of self-restraint to keep from rolling my eyes. "In a manner of speaking, yes. He delivered a key piece of evidence though." The secret pun amuses me.

Bristol makes a little fist and pulls it down as she lifts her knee. "Sweet. That cat rules." She waves and stalks out the front door.

Fan clubs. Stepbrothers. Stepmothers. What is happening in my life?

CHAPTER 18

SOMETIMES THE QUIET before the storm is more unsettling than the storm itself. I swallow all of my theories and hypotheses and run out the front door toward the station. Once inside, I find there's no deputy at the front desk, and the bullpen is empty. Marching through the silence, I pause in Erick's doorway.

He looks up and shakes his head. "You were right about everything. I don't know how you do it, Moon? Paulsen ended up taking the call, and she's bringing McGrail in now. Gilbert and Johnson had to run that black SUV off the road, and one of the occupants pulled a gun. Johnson was able to de-escalate the situation and bring the perpetrators into custody without having to fire his weapon. That's always a good day, as far as I'm concerned."

Sinking onto one of the uncomfortable wooden chairs, I cross my legs and make little circles with my foot. "Eli just turned eighteen, right?"

"Yeah, why?"

"I guess it doesn't matter. I mean, he killed someone."

Erick leans forward. "Who told you that?"

"What do you mean?"

"Well, Paulsen said he started confessing as soon as she put him in handcuffs, and despite the fact that she read him his Miranda warning, he wouldn't shut up. But how do you know?"

"It's a long story. Honestly, I'm not trying to hide anything. I never really suspected Mr. Lee, and the body dump theory didn't ring true for me. Even if there wasn't much blood, moving a body across the snow . . . I just couldn't figure out how the killer did it."

He leans back and taps the eraser of his pencil on the desk. "They groom the tracks every morning before the event. So if the plow driver didn't see the blood, it could have easily been scraped to the side. That part never concerned me. The precision of the wound was what made Mr. Lee such a strong suspect."

"True. Do you think Eli knew what he was doing?"

Paulsen's gruff voice echoes down the hallway

as she yanks her prisoner toward Interrogation Room Two.

Erick glances across the desk and tilts his head. "Looks like we're about to find out."

She sticks her head in the doorway. "He's all yours, Sheriff. Shouldn't be too difficult to get him to sign a confession. He's been runnin' his mouth since I threw him in the back of the cruiser."

"Thanks, Paulsen. Can you follow up with Johnson and Gilbert? They might need some help with those traffickers and the warrant."

"10-4."

He walks around the desk, sighs, and heads across the hallway to question the suspect.

I take a beat before slipping into the observation room.

Eli is a disaster. His dark hair is greasy and un-kempt, purple-black bags hang beneath his sunken eyes, and his sallow skin screams insomnia. The only thing more heartbreaking than his appearance is his story.

Sheriff Harper presses record on the device and begins the interview. "Please state your name."

The young man's hands shake, and he digs ner-vously at invisible dirt under his fingernails. "Elijah McGrail."

Once the particulars are on the record, the interrogation begins in earnest. "Mr. McGrail, did you kill Stanley Jablonski?"

"I guess. I don't know what happened. I was up in the pit tent, tweaking some settings on my sled. They were arguing so loud, I couldn't ignore it, you know?"

Erick nods.

"Then Jawbone got on his sled and took off, and Lee's dad stormed out." He stops and rubs his throat with his left hand. "Can I get some water, man?"

Harper places the request over the radio, and Paulsen delivers a cup of agua.

"Anything else, Sheriff? Is he trying to lawyer up?"

Erick slides the cup of water toward the prisoner. "He's declined to have counsel present. Thanks, Paulsen."

She shrugs at the dismissive tone, but exits the interrogation room.

Eli drains the cup of water in one go. "I didn't mean to kill him."

The sheriff leans forward. "Eli, you took a screwdriver from Mr. Lee's toolbox. That indicates premeditation. Crimes of passion and weapons of opportunity go out the window when evidence of a plan is uncovered. Trying to frame Mr. Lee is evidence of a plan."

"Well, they were arguing, you know? I . . . I just

can't afford to lose. My dad's out of work, my mom's homebound . . . My prize money was keeping us afloat. If Jawbone coaches Freddy Priest, I'm screwed. If I lose my sponsors, we lose everything."

The word "sponsors" tickles something in my memory, and I activate a psychic instant replay. The helmet. When I first met Eli, I noticed his helmet was covered with sponsor emblems, but now that I can slow down the image and focus on each one, a new detail emerges. A World Wildlife Fund sticker and two PETA decals. Eli is an animal rights activist.

Erick presses to get the interrogation back on track. "Tell me what happened after you picked up the screwdriver."

Eli's eyes seem to glaze over as he relives the events of Friday night. He waited until Jawbone parked his sled at the bottom of the drag tracks and started his inspection on foot.

"He had his helmet on, so he didn't hear me walking up behind him. As I got closer, I realized what a big guy he was. I figured he'd turn and see me. I thought he might kill me. I feared for my life."

"Mr. McGrail, I believe it's dishonest to admit to premeditation of murder and then try to blame the victim for the crime. Please continue describing the events that occurred after you approached Mr. Jablonski on the drag track."

Eli wrings his hands and struggles to get the last drops of liquid from the bottom of the cup. "I panicked. Like I said, I thought he might turn and try something, you know? So I just held up the screwdriver and lunged at him. It slipped in right under the back of the helmet and . . ."

The sheriff draws out the last few details, and Eli admits to shoving Jablonski off the side of the track, cleaning up any blood from the snow, and making sure the body was well covered. He also admits to moving Jablonski's sled into the tent and placing the murder weapon back into Mr. Lee's toolbox. He claims it wasn't to create a frame up, but Sheriff Harper doesn't seem to buy what he's selling.

"One last thing." Erick sighs and leans back. "Why break into the taxidermy shed?"

Eli's jaw clenches and I can feel waves of righteous indignation roll off him. "I always hated that he stuffed those poor animals. After Jawbone's body was discovered, I panicked. I thought if I staged a break-in it would muddy the waters. And, like, as soon as I saw the condor and stuff . . . I couldn't let anyone profit off them, you know?"

Sheriff Harper shakes his head. "Mr. McGrail, I'm placing you under arrest on suspicion of first-degree murder." Erick offers him another opportunity to call an attorney, but Eli refuses. Part of him continues to defend his actions as some form of self-defense, while the other half begs to be punished for a crime he can't believe he committed.

The satisfaction of catching the killer is missing for me. Eli is only a couple of years older than Stellen. I don't want to let myself think about it.

Life is full of disparity. I'm sorry he put himself in that situation, and that actions have consequences, and too often people seem to forget that.

Erick hands off the prisoner to Paulsen and she marches him back to the holding cells.

The handle on the observation room door twists, and the handsome sheriff steps through. "What a sad story, eh?"

I nod my agreement and sigh. "It's always hard when the bad guy isn't all that bad."

"Yeah. Misguided. Suffering from poor judgment. But definitely not malevolent. Makes me double glad you and your dad stepped in to help Stellen. It's about the best we could have hoped for in a pretty terrible situation."

I hold out my hand and wiggle my fingers.

Erick steps forward, takes my hand, and pulls me close. "Thanks for your help on the case."

"That's what I do. What about the traffickers?"

"That's gonna take some unraveling. We're waiting on a second, more inclusive warrant, but Johnson said initial inspection of the property revealed several more animals, and a ton of cash. We're hoping to scare them into testifying against the rest of the ring. Obviously they didn't pull a hawksbill sea turtle out of the great lake. Someone's getting these animals into the country, and into their hands. I'm happy to shut down this end of the operation, but I'd be much happier to destroy the entire thing."

"Yeah, that would be fantastic. Hey, what's the update on Trey? I heard he could possibly have been paralyzed or suffered brain damage? Is that true?"

He pushes me away slightly and smiles down at me. "Oh, you heard that, did you? Do you happen to remember where you were or who you heard that from, Miss Moon?"

Gulp. "I plead the fifth."

He squeezes me close and kisses me firmly. "You may need more than amendments to protect you."

Tingles from head to toe. Weak knees. Inability to catch a breath.

He whispers in my ear. "Sounds like your *ward* is moving into new digs across the alley. Does that mean you'll be all by your lonesome in that apartment?"

And I'm dead.

His strong arms keep me from melting into a puddle of love-struck goo.

"I have to focus on this wedding. Don't try to distract me, or whatever."

"Fair enough. But the wedding will be over and done with Thursday night. You'd better start working on a new set of excuses."

"I just remembered, I have a dress fitting." Pulling away unceremoniously, I rush out of the observation room and steady myself on the wall.

There had better be some real-life magic in New Year's resolutions, because I'm running out of ways to resist that utterly irresistible man.

Running back toward my bookshop, I wish I had a dress fitting. The probability of Mr. Gustafson having the necessary magicks to squeeze these hips into that piece of couture is low. I best run over to wedding central and see if there's anything I can do for the bride. When the elevator doors open on the first floor, my new stepbrother looks as shocked to see me as I am to see him.

"Hey, I was just coming to your place."

I take a magnanimous bow. "Great minds think alike. What d'you need, buddy?"

He chews mercilessly on the edge of his fingernail and steps into the marble elevator lobby. "Um, do you think that . . . Would it be weird . . .?"

Finally, my resurrected psychic senses and my mood ring unite. I gaze down at the tingling image and grab the clairsentient message from thin air. "Would you like to go visit Trey Lee in the hospital?"

For a moment his face is blank of all expression, and then he tilts his head. "Cool trick. Can you teach me?"

"It's hardly a trick, young man." We share a little chuckle, and for a moment I have a glimpse of what it must be like to be Silas Willoughby. "Seriously, do you want to go?"

"Yeah. If you think it's okay."

"It's fine. Follow me to the Moonmobile."

I hear him snickering behind me as we cross the lobby of the empty foundation, now closed for the holidays.

My ring tingles warmly on my left hand, and I flick my eyes over in time to catch a glimpse of Crystal floating in the glassy mists as we load into the Jeep. Deep breaths. Deep breaths. "Hey, something happened out at your house, you know, when you took off in my vehicle."

He looks down at his feet. "Sorry about that. It was a stupid thing to do. I'm glad your Jeep wasn't trashed."

This amazing kid never ceases to amaze. "No sweat. That's not what I was talking about. When you left me alone to read the journal . . . she appeared."

His head whip pans my direction, and his expression is a heartbreaking mashup of hope and loss. "I missed seeing my mom? Can we go back out there? Do you think she'd appear again?"

Shaking my head, I struggle to stuff the emotions and speak. "I don't think she'll be making any more visits. She finally crossed over."

He chokes on his emotions and wipes his nose with the back of his hand. "Why?"

"I told her about your father's death and our friendship, and the adoption. She seemed so happy that you were surrounded by people who cared about you."

"But I don't want her to cross over. I have so much to tell her."

"She had a message for you too."

His tear-streaked face turns toward me, and I have to pull to the side of the street. "I told her about your apprenticeship and plans for vet school, and how you saved Pye. She called you her stellar Stellen. She said she always knew you were special." My fight with my own tears fails, and I take a minute to steady my voice. "Most importantly, she said it broke her heart to have to leave before she got to see you grow up. I think my update brought her the comfort she needed to get closure."

He sobs into his hands and sniffles. "I miss her so much."

"I understand. I'll tell you what Silas told me. We have to speak the names of the dead. If we stop talking about them, that's when they're truly forgotten. As long as you remember Crystal and tell her stories, she'll live on through you. It's hard, and some days it really sucks, but you're strong, like me. We'll get through it together, all right, Bro-seph?"

My Jack Black reference tickles his funny bone, and he smiles through the tears. "Thanks for telling me." He exhales loudly and presses his hands on his thighs. "Crystal was the best mom. The best, you know?"

"I know." Reaching over, I place my hand on his and give him a reassuring squeeze. I pull back onto Gunnison and continue toward the hospital.

"Tomorrow's the big wedding, right?"

And I thought I had cornered the market on "left field" questions. I let the question hang for a moment. "Yeah. I'm thrilled for my dad. He's been through a lot."

Stellen draws a tic-tac-toe on the frost inside the window. "Seems like Amaryllis really cares about him. Some people are just lucky in love, you know?"

Oh, the days of teenage angst. So near, and yet so far. "Don't worry, bro. High school is the last place on earth you should worry about fitting in. You're destined to be a great-looking guy, and you already have a heart of gold. That's a pretty irresistible combination."

His finger delicately connects the diagonal row of "Xs" and he smirks. "Like Sheriff Harper?"

Unexpectedly blushing a deep scarlet, I clear my throat and briefly choke. "Mind your own business. How can you already be this good at being an annoying little brother?"

He shrugs. "I got skills."

We struggle to stifle our giggles and strike the appropriate mood as we stroll into the hospital to request directions to Trey's room.

Outside the door of the private recovery room, Stellen and I exchange a shrug. Mr. Lee is asleep in a chair next to the bed, and Mrs. Lee is whispering softly into her phone.

Stellen shakes his head. "I don't want to interrupt."

"Hey, the worst they can say is no. I'll handle it." Knocking softly on the door, I offer a friendly smile through the narrow pane of glass.

Mrs. Lee fumbles with her phone, ends the call, and walks toward the door. "Hi, are you friends of Trey?"

I smile and offer my hand. "I'm Mitzy Moon, and this is Stellen Jablonski."

The color drains from her face and she tilts her head in that all-too-predictable way. "Oh dear, I'm so sorry for your loss."

Stellen swallows and struggles to find his voice. "Thanks. My dad was really proud of Trey. I just wanted to see if he was okay."

She waves us in, and we stand awkwardly at the end of the boy's bed.

"My husband's been here twenty-four hours a day since the accident. Well, except—Never mind."

Gently placing my hand on her arm, I offer a bit of good news. "They've arrested Eli McGrail for Stan Jablonski's murder. I'm so sorry Mr. Lee was ever a suspect."

She breathes a tremendous sigh of relief and tears leak from the corners of her eyes. "Thank God." She looks over at Stellen and leans toward me to whisper, "What's going to happen to him? I remember when his mother passed away. He's all alone, isn't he?"

I give her a brief recap of the best-case-scenario outcome for Stellen. She's pleased with the news.

"Two days ago, the doctor told us Trey had suffered a serious spinal injury. He said the helmet had protected him from any brain damage, but the prognosis for him ever walking again was in the single digits."

Pressing my hand to my heart, I exhale as Stellen moves closer to the sleeping boy.

"The lawyer from the hospital came and wanted us to sign a bunch of papers. Such a strange little man and so bossy."

The hairs on the back of my neck tingle. "He came to your hospital room?"

"He gave me a huge stack of papers and waved us outside to review them. For some reason, I didn't feel like I could say no to him."

My heart is already swelling with gratitude, because, psychic or not, I am predicting the end of her story.

"When we came back in, he actually had his hands on Trey. My husband was furious. The man completely ignored us. He collected the papers and disappeared. Don't you think that's strange?"

"Very strange. And how is Trey doing today?"

She rubs her hand across her forehead and sighs. "The doctors can't explain it. They came in to run the usual tests, and Trey moved his feet." Mrs. Lee covers her mouth with her hand, and I pat her back reassuringly.

"That's wonderful. I'm sure he'll make a full recovery."

She nods and smiles. "I know. At first the doctor was speechless, but eventually he said the same thing. Just that miraculous healing thing that kids have, I guess. I'm not going to ask any questions. If Trey couldn't race, I have no—"

Trey opens his eyes and looks up at Stellen. "Hey, man. What's up?"

Stellen shrugs and looks at the floor. "Just making sure you're gonna get back on your sled, you know?"

Trey smiles, but is unable to nod his head in the cervical brace. "Tell your dad not to worry. I'll be back next season, and I'm gonna win the championship for him."

Stellen nibbles his fingernail and nods. "Totally, dude. Totally." His tender green eyes search me out, and I answer with a subtle nod.

"Thank you for taking the time to see us, Mrs. Lee. Stellen and I really should get going."

She sniffles and smiles at Stellen. "Thank you for stopping by. He's on a lot of medication, but I'll make sure to remind him you were here."

We smile politely and make our way out.

As we drive back to Stellen's new home, he places a tentative hand on my shoulder. "Thanks. I don't know why, but somehow it makes me feel better to know that he's going to be okay."

I wish I could tell him the role I suspect Silas Willoughby played in the boy's recovery, but that's not my secret to tell. "Me too. Me too."

CHAPTER 19

THE BOOKSHOP HAS BEEN TRANSFORMED into a magical fantasy. All the oak tables are carefully repositioned down the curving arms of the mezzanine and camouflaged with layers of white tulle and shimmering fairy lights. Despite Twiggy's endless protestations, Amaryllis and I eventually convinced her to give in to the wedding juggernaut. Crisp rows of seating fill the first floor, and the small dais, which we use for fundraisers and author events, has been completely transformed with a delicate snowflake-and-fairy-light-encrusted archway and mountains of fake snow.

My film school experience actually came in handy when it was time to devise a method of delivering an indoor cascade of snowflakes following the completion of the vows. Stellen used his father's huge network of suppliers to procure the realistic-looking plastic snowflakes and helped me wire the fancy delivery tubes to the ceiling. My natural clumsiness would have certainly ended with my death or severe injury, whereas the nimble young lad scurried up ladders and balanced precariously three stories in the air, with no sign of fear. Miraculously, everything was in place in time for the rehearsal.

To be clear, the rehearsal was not without its hiccups.

Grams was entirely unwilling to abide by the rules I'd set, and she kept popping in to weep uncontrollably at the most inconvenient times. Stellen's poker face is improving, but he's still rather excited by his ability to see ghosts, and his frequent outbursts and pointing derailed the proceedings multiple times. The confused justice of the peace simply chalked it up to the young man's grief.

However, the day has finally dawned and my newly adopted brother and I are eager to fulfill our roles. I as the plucky maid of honor, and he as my father's best man.

The bride and groom planned their post-nuptial march to wend through the faux snowfall indoors, down the aisle, and out the front door of the bookshop, where they will likely be met with genuine snowfall as they make their way to the reception area behind the bookshop. Hundreds of twinkling lights line the pathway and surround the eating area and dance floor. Propane heaters were trucked in from as far away as Grand Falls to make sure the attendees stay above freezing despite the predicted subzero temperatures.

While the prospect of my father's wedding is, of course, an exciting event, the piece I'm truly looking forward to comes at the reception. I'm told that each and every citizen of Pin Cherry Harbor traditionally purchases their own supply of fireworks, and at midnight everyone lights their horde simultaneously. The dark sky becomes a beautiful cacophony of lights, and the scene warms hearts and souls across the northland.

Time to start the official wedding day. Now that Stellen has moved into the spare room at the penthouse, I opted for the settee and gave Amaryllis my bed so she and my father could spend the pre-wedding night apart. However, Pyewacket is taking far more room than he's entitled to, and the crick in my back wakes me up sooner than I'd like.

"Amaryllis?" My voice is barely more than a whisper. Pyewacket stretches out one of his large tan paws to cover my mouth, in what he'd like to pretend is an accident.

"Oh my gosh, I'm so glad you're finally awake. I've been lying here for at least two hours."

Amaryllis flicks back the heavy down comforter and sits upright. "Should we grab some breakfast before we start the massive effort of whipping this—" she jumps up and gestures comically to her ratty flannel pajamas "—into shape?"

Slipping out from under the weight of a lazy half-wild caracal, I yawn and stretch. "You look amazing, as usual. But I absolutely need breakfast, and at least a gallon of coffee."

I take a quick turn in the bathroom and get dressed while Amaryllis washes and moisturizes her face like a grownup.

The diner is more than half full, and Tally's daughter is helping her mother take care of the flood of tourons who are visiting the great lake over the holidays. "Hi, ladies. I'll be right over with your coffee. I'm sure Odell already has your breakfasts on the grill."

We both nod our thanks and my clairsentience picks up on a wave of nerves from my tablemate. "Everything all right? Just normal nerves, or is there something else going on?"

"Just worried about the ceremony. My father is recovering surprisingly well from his heart attack, but he's not able to travel. Which is fine. I'd much rather have him well than risk his health for a short walk down the aisle. But—"

"I'm sure Silas would be honored to stand in, if you're all right with that."

Her hands shoot across the table. She grips my fingers and squeezes them so tightly a small squeak escapes my mouth as I ask, "Do you want me to ask him for you?"

"Would you? I know you keep telling me what a sweet old man he is, but every time I think about asking him, all I can picture is his disappointed face during my second year in law school when I got a 'B-' on my history of torte law brief." Her nervous laughter reddens her cheeks.

"I keep forgetting that he was one of your professors. You poor thing. Trust me, I've been on the receiving end of that look many times. I won't say I'm immune to it, but I'm happy to endure it for someone else's benefit. Especially you." I squeeze her hand and an enormous sigh of relief escapes her lips as she leans back against the red-vinyl bench seat.

"Well, that's a load off. I think I might actually be able to eat my breakfast now."

Right on time, Tally approaches the table with our food. She starts to push a plate in front of me, but stops halfway to the table. "Wait? You both— I never realized!"

Amaryllis and I exchange a shrug.

Tally sets our plates on the table and an entire *Three Stooges* sequence plays out.

I look at her plate.

She looks at my plate.

Tally looks back and forth between the two of us, until finally our eyes meet and the three of us laugh heartily.

I wave to Odell through the orders-up window, and he gives me a quick spatula salute before he continues filling orders.

Amaryllis holds up her coffee cup. "Cheers to the chorizo sisters!"

I pick up my mug, clink it against hers, and let the warmth of family fill my heart.

Back at the apartment, Grams is insisting on helping Amaryllis with her hair. After at least fifteen minutes of playing otherworld interpreter, I manage to convince Grams that having the wedding at the bookshop is her win for the year, and she should be ecstatic that Amaryllis has a trusted stylist showing up at two o'clock to create the hairstyle of the bride's dreams. Grams vanishes with a loud, self-indulgent pop, and I spend another ten minutes reassuring Amaryllis that she made the right choice and the motto is absolutely, "Her day, her way."

Caterers, florists, cake creators, and general delivery personnel are scurrying in and out of the bookshop all day.

However, my volunteer employee, Twiggy, is one hundred percent in control of all the main-floor shenanigans.

When my father makes an unscheduled visit, Twiggy's half-panicked voice crackles over the intercom. "Hey, kid, your dad's here, and I'm not letting him upstairs for the life of me. So you better get down here before I hafta put him in a chokehold."

Amaryllis laughs so hard she snorts. "I don't believe in superstitions, Mitzy. If it's important, he can come upstairs."

I throw my hands in the air as though it's an old-fashioned stickup. "No way! There were a lot of things I didn't believe in before I came to Pin Cherry, and I've discovered that most of them actually exist. So I'm not going to push my luck on this important day. I'll go take care of this, and under no circumstances will I allow him to come upstairs. Besides, your stylist will be here any minute."

She smiles proudly and winks. "I'm not even married yet, and you're the best stepdaughter anyone could ever ask for."

A ball of emotion clogs my throat. I can't keep images of my mother from popping into my head.

Amaryllis must be able to read my face as clear

as a street sign, because she hops up from the scalloped-back chair and hurries to my side. "I'm sorry. I know today is hard for you. I wasn't trying to flaunt it or anything. I just want you to know how special I think you are, and how grateful I am to be part of your and your father's life."

Her kindness only forces a fresh flood of emotion, and I have to swipe salty drops from my cheeks. "It's fine. I'm super happy for you and Dad. My mother was definitely taken from me too soon, but that doesn't mean I don't want you and Jacob to be happy. You've changed his life. I can see, and sense, how much he loves you." Before I can prepare myself, she throws her arms around me and squeezes me in a bear hug.

"Thank you, Mitzy. Thank you for saying that."

I struggle to free myself from the cage of emotions. "I better get downstairs. I'm pretty sure Twiggy could take Dad, but I don't think we want to see that match on this day."

Amaryllis's tinkling laughter trails behind me and is finally cut off as the bookcase door slides closed.

At the bottom of the spiral staircase, my father is nose to nose with Twiggy.

"Easy, Dad. It's bad luck for you to see the bride on the wedding day. Just tell me what you need, and I'll take care of everything."

He rakes a nervous hand through his hair and his breath is coming in quick gasps. "I lost the ring. I picked it up from the jewelers last week, before they closed for the holidays, and I must've left it in the pocket of my pants. Maybe it fell out . . . I don't know! I can't find it anywhere."

"I bet I know someone who can find it." I give my father a huge over-obvious wink as I wiggle a finger back toward myself.

He sighs with relief. "Right. Get yourself over to my apartment tout de suite."

I step over the chain at the bottom of the stairs and scowl at Twiggy. "You have to unhook that. You can't expect Amaryllis to step over the "No Admittance" chain in a wedding gown."

Twiggy crosses her arms and kicks the toe of her biker boot on the bottom step. "As soon as the security gets here. I'll unhook the chain."

I gasp. "He's my boyfriend, not a gun for hire!"

She shrugs silently, turns my shoulders toward my father, and gives me a gentle shove.

Grumbling under my breath all the way across the alley, I can't ignore my father's chuckling.

"Don't worry, Mitzy, she's messing with you. I'm sure it's one of the other deputies. Indignantly jumping to conclusions is an unfortunate Duncan trait. I apologize for passing it on to you. But allow me to pass on a little wisdom, too. There are a great many things in this life that are out of your control. What other people think about you is absolutely one of them. I'm sure you want to protect yourself from the pain of losing someone you love, but keeping Erick at arms' length and refusing to trust him with the *whole* truth, will turn out to be a self-fulfilling prophecy. You're right in thinking he might not understand the psychic thing. But if you don't give him a chance, you'll always wonder what could have been."

There's a raw pain in my father's eyes, and I know he's thinking about the time he came to Arizona and saw my mother and me enjoying an ice cream. He chose to walk away that day. He thought I'd be better off without him. Who knows what would've happened if he had joined us instead of disappearing from our lives? Maybe this is my ice-cream-shop moment with Erick. If I don't trust him . . . if I don't walk over there, sit down, and ask to share his ice cream, I could drive away the one person I truly let myself care about since my mom died. "I hear what you're saying, Dad. I'll take it under advisement. Now, let's find that ring."

The immediate gratification of using my psychic powers to find something that means so much to my father, in less than three minutes, gives me a lovely boost of confidence. "You're welcome."

He squeezes me and lifts me up off the ground.

"Have I told you that you are literally the best daughter in the entire world?"

"Oh, sorry. I didn't mean to interrupt."

My father drops me on the floor and both of our heads turn toward Stellen. "You didn't interrupt anything, little brother."

He blushes and looks away. "Mr. Duncan, are you sure you want me to be in the wedding party?"

Jacob strides across the tiger-maple flooring and puts a hand on the boy's shoulder. "First of all, I'd like you to call me Jacob. And I said it before, but I'll say it again, I'm honored to have you stand beside me on such an important day. You're a strong kid, and the fact you're the only other person I know who can see ghosts is a clear sign that you were meant to be part of this family." He slips his arm around the boy's shoulder and turns toward me. "What is it that you always say, Mitzy? The family of our choosing?"

I nod and join them in an impromptu family hug. "All right, boys. Let's make sure Amaryllis has the most perfect wedding in history, deal?"

They both nod, and we all put our hands in a circle like a small sports team. "Best wedding ever, on three. One. Two. Three!" We throw our hands up in the air and laugh.

"I better get back. It's going to take a small army

and a large shoehorn to get me into that brides-maid's dress."

Stellen snickers, exactly as I imagine a real baby brother would, and I punch him playfully on the shoulder before running to the elevator.

CHAPTER 20

TWIGGY HANDS me a garment bag and I glare at her as I struggle over the chain and start up the circular staircase.

"Good luck with the dress, doll. Let me know if you need any safety pins or duct tape." She cackles happily as she struts over to check the florist's credentials.

When the secret door to the apartment slides open, Amaryllis calls from the bathroom. "Jacob, is that you?"

"Nope. It's only me."

"Everything okay?"

"Absolutely perfect. Do I put on my dress now, or is it better to wait till after the hairdo?"

The stylist steps out of the bathroom, takes a sip of bubbly, and sizes me up. "Hair first. We're probably going to need a lot of product, and I'd hate to get anything on the dress."

"Copy that." The hours disappear as we primp and bobby pin, and apply more layers of makeup than I've worn in my entire life. When the moment finally comes to cross my fingers and wedge into the dress, both Amaryllis and I are speechless.

"It fits you like a glove!" She blinks her false eyelashes and claps her hands.

I turn in front of the mirror and adjust the faux-fur trim on my shoulders.

"This can't possibly be the same dress?"

Amaryllis whistles. "Enjoy the win, Mitzy. And you might want another mimosa. I regret to inform you, I lost the shoe battle with your grandmother."

I roll my eyes and search the room, but Grams has cleverly hidden. "Do I even want to know?"

She leads me into the closet and reveals a strappy pair of silver heels somewhere in the four-to five-inch range. My fur-trimmed shoulders sag, and Amaryllis gives me an encouraging pat on the back. "You only have to wear them for the ceremony. If you change into high-tops for the reception, I'll never tell."

I laugh too loud and too long. "You severely underestimate the machinations of a vengeful fashion diva."

Once again, the flurry of activity swallows time,

and before I can adequately admire the magical alterations of Mr. Gustafson, the music swells and I'm walking across the Rare Books Loft in my perfectly fitted gown.

The white fur hugs my shoulders, and I'm grateful I didn't finish my mimosa as I circle down the wrought-iron steps and all eyes turn. Thankfully the chain is unhooked at the bottom, and Deputy Johnson is the actual security guard.

As I stride down the aisle toward the glittering archway, a familiar face catches my eye.

Erick makes a point of looking me up and down before nodding his heartfelt approval.

My cheeks flush to match my dress as I join my father on stage.

The tune shifts from "Winter Wonderland" to the traditional bride's march. Although I helped her into her gown, and observed the three hours of preparation, when Amaryllis stops at the top of the staircase, I gasp along with the rest of the guests.

Her auburn curls cascade down her back, and a sparkling winter princess's tiara sits atop her head like a delicate ice sculpture. The crown is festooned with holly berries, pine sprigs, and snowdrops. Her gorgeous bell-sleeved gown sparkles in the intimate lighting, and I can barely tear my eyes away from her descent in time to see my father brush a tear from his cheek.

The "I dos" are said, and the groom kisses the bride. Mr. and Mrs. Duncan descend the stage under a cascade of lightly falling snowflakes.

Guests ooh and ahh.

The happy couple stops behind the last row, so Twiggy can help the bride into her stunning white faux-fur cloak. They proceed to the outdoor reception area, and Stellen, handsome beyond his years in his white tuxedo and red bowtie, offers me his elbow.

We march out to the cheers and celebration of the crowd, who soon join us outdoors.

I help myself to the signature cocktail of brandy-infused mulled cider, and unabashedly take my seat at the head table. Food first, dancing later.

The seared elk medallions with garlic mashed potatoes and roasted root vegetables are spectacular.

The five-tier chocolate wedding cake brushed with Chambord liqueur and filled with dark chocolate ganache and raspberry preserves is divine.

And the propane heaters are life saving.

When it's time for the bride to throw her bouquet, Stellen nearly drags me out to the dance floor to join the growing group of single ladies.

I ease my way toward the back of the crowd, sincerely hoping that more eager, more coordinated women win the evening.

Amaryllis turns her back to us and, as her beautiful poinsettia, snowdrop, and pinecone bouquet floats through the air, I see the expectant faces of the women around me tracking its motion.

A tall blonde in the front row looks to be in perfect position, but at the last moment the bouquet takes a sharp turn and practically forces itself into my hands.

I immediately suspect Grams, and my eyes shoot up to the apartment windows.

She's whirling with glee like a mad dervish, but she can't leave the apartment. I suppose that places her in the clear.

Awkwardly clutching the birch-bark-wrapped bouquet grip, I smile my apologies to the disappointed faces around me.

The crowd parts to reveal the self-satisfied smirk of my mentor. His role as surrogate father of the bride may not have won him any awards, but his transmutation of the elements that altered the bouquet's trajectory will earn him high praise from my interfering Ghost-ma.

The music swells for the bride's first dance, and I scurry toward the sidelines.

The dapper Erick Harper intercepts my escape, twirls me back onto the dance floor, and winks at Stellen.

My conniving little stepbrother is enjoying a hearty chuckle and a second piece of cake.

"You know I'm a terrible dancer, Erick."

He twirls me out, spins me back, and dips me. "And you know—I'm not."

As he plants a memorable kiss on my lips, I drop the bouquet and possibly lose consciousness for a second.

Without missing a beat, he swoops me back to my feet with one hand and scoops up the floral arrangement with the other.

"I hope you believe in tradition, Moon." He offers me the bouquet.

I open my mouth to protest, but the sight of Deputy Johnson grooving at the edge of the dance floor sends a sharp shock up my spine.

"Mitzy, are you okay?"

Peeling my eyes away from the wandering deputy, I stare blankly at Erick as the mood ring on my left hand burns with an unholy fire. "I have to find Silas."

Hiking up the skirts of my magnificent dress, I tempt fate and run in heels.

As though he senses the disturbance, Silas meets me at the edge of the dance floor and offers his elbow. "What has transpired?"

"I'm not sure. I saw Deputy Johnson standing at the edge of the dance floor, instead of guarding the

Rare Books Loft." I lift my mood-ringed finger and shrug.

My mentor's bushy eyebrows arch, and he increases the pace. For a man who looks to be in his late seventies or early eighties, there's a strength that lurks beneath the surface.

We round the corner and rush inside. Unsurprisingly, he reaches the top of the spiral stairs before me and calls down, "Mitzy, did you move *Loca Sine Lumine, Loca Sine Lege?*"

"Is that the book that just came in? The one about places without light or laws?"

A worried sigh is his only reply.

When I reach the top stair my eyes dart toward the candle handle, and the shelf where the new book should be resting. "It's gone!"

"Indeed." He smooths his mustache with a thumb and forefinger. "There's nothing that can be done tonight. We must return to the festivities, properly admonish Deputy Johnson, and allow your father and his new bride to enjoy their evening."

"I know the book was rare, and I'm sure valuable, but is it dangerous?"

Silas takes my hand and pats it with fatherly patience. "Anything can be dangerous in the wrong hands, my dear. Let us return to the party. If I'm not mistaken, you left a very confused sheriff alone on the dance floor, holding a bouquet of flowers."

My eyes widen, and I stifle a giggle. "I'll blame it on Ghost-ma. He wanted to be in the inner circle, right?"

We both wait with bated breath, but no apparition rockets through the wall.

Silas's cheeks redden, and his round belly shakes with laughter. "You're fortunate she is otherwise occupied with her observation of the reception."

We return to the dance floor, where Erick is already dressing down Deputy Johnson for his dereliction of duty.

The young rookie shuffles back toward the bookshop, and I slip in to make my apologies.

Sheriff Harper cocks his head to the side and scrunches up his face. "If you keep running out on me when I'm using my best moves, I'm going to get a complex."

"Sorry. Ghost business." I jerk a thumb toward the windows. "It won't happen again—tonight."

He waves to Stellen, who raises the bouquet as though it is a glass of champagne, and the young man offers me a brotherly wink.

Erick smiles. "I gave it to him for safekeeping. Can we finish our dance?"

Before I can offer up my prepared litany of excuses, the clock strikes midnight and almost-Canada bursts to life with a flurry of fireworks and cheers.

Watching the reflection of sparkly explosions in Erick's deep-blue eyes holds me in a trance.

If I had words, I wouldn't know what to do with them.

This moment, this feeling, this is me—living my best life.

End of Book 11

A NOTE FROM TRIXIE

Thank you to each and every one of you! Another case solved! I'll keep writing them if you keep reading . . .

The best part of "living" in Pin Cherry Harbor continues to be feedback from my early readers. Thank you to my alpha readers/cheerleaders, Angel and Michael. HUGE thanks to my fantastic beta readers who continue to give me extremely useful and honest feedback: Veronica McIntyre and Nadine Peterse-Vrijhof. And big "small town" hugs to the world's best ARC Team – Trixie's Mystery ARC Detectives!

Another thing I'm truly grateful for is my editor, Philip Newey. Thank you for the elegant "fluttering page" solution. I'd also like to give some heartfelt thanks to Brooke for her tireless proofreading! Any errors are my own, as my outdated version of Word insists on showing me only what it likes and when it feels so moved.

FUN FACT: I have actually driven a snowmobile across a frozen lake!

My favorite quote from this case: "Poor man. The hips of Mitzy Moon may be the end of his winning streak." ~ Mitzy

I'm currently writing book thirteen in the Mitzy Moon Mysteries series, and I think I may just live in Pin Cherry Harbor forever. Mitzy, Grams, and Pyewacket got into plenty of trouble in book one, *Fries and Alibis*. But I'd have to say that book three, *Wings and Broken Things*, is when most readers say the series becomes unputdownable.

I hope you'll continue to hang out with us.

Trixie Silvertale (December 2020)

Mitzy Moon Mysteries 12

When a disappearing dog leads to a decades-old feud, will this psychic sleuth settle the score?

Mitzy Moon is bending over backward to be a good big sister. Spending a day at the pet invention convention seems harmless enough. But when puppy love turns into vanishing canines and a vengeful ghost, she'll have to bend a few laws before more furry friends are spirited away...

Ignoring the handsome sheriff's warnings about evidence that cuts both ways, Mitzy's desperation drives her to make daring decisions. Unfortunately, one crime leads to two and her carelessness puts Ghost-ma and her interfering feline in danger. And with her family threatened by dangerous powers, her dreams of a happy ending could become a ghastly nightmare.

Can Mitzy save the pooch and her grand-mother, or will she be forced to make a deadly choice?

Hearts and Dark Arts is the twelfth book in the hilarious paranormal cozy mystery series, Mitzy Moon Mysteries. If you like snarky heroines, super-natural twists, and a dash of romance, then you'll love Trixie Silvertale's madcap caper.

Buy *Hearts and Dark Arts* to undo the Valen-tine's mayhem today!

Grab yours here!
readerlinks.com/l/861835

Scan this QR Code with the camera on your phone. You'll be taken right to the Mitzy Moon Mysteries series page. You can easily grab any mysteries you've missed!

Once you're in the Club, you'll also be the first to receive updates from Pin Cherry Harbor and access to giveaways, new release announcements, behind-the-scenes secrets, and much more!

Scan this QR Code with the camera on your phone. You'll be taken right to the page to join the Club!

THANK YOU!

Trying out a new book is always a risk and I'm thankful that you rolled the dice with Mitzy Moon. If you loved the book, the sweetest thing you can do (*even sweeter than pin cherry pie à la mode*) is to leave a review so that other readers will take a chance on Mitzy and the gang.

Don't feel you have to write a book report. A brief comment like, "Can't wait to read the next book in this series!" will help potential readers make their choice.

★★★★★
Leave a quick review HERE
https://readerlinks.com/l/1493022
★★★★★

Thank you kindly, and I'll see you in Pin Cherry Harbor!

Trixie Silvertale grew up reading an endless supply of Lilian Jackson Braun, Hardy Boys, and Nancy Drew novels. She loves the amateur sleuths in cozy mysteries and obsesses about all things paranormal. Those two passions unite in her Mitzy Moon Mysteries, and she's thrilled to write them and share them with you.

When she's not consumed by writing, she bakes to fuel her creative engine and pulls weeds in her herb garden to clear her head (*and sometimes she pulls out her hair, but mostly weeds*).

Greetings are welcome:
trixie@trixiesilvertale.com

BB bookbub.com/authors/trixie-silvertale

f facebook.com/TrixieSilvertale

instagram.com/trixiesilvertale

Made in the USA
Las Vegas, NV
15 October 2021